S.R. SOTOLONGO

The Ballad of Abigail Lambert

First edition

ISBN: 979-8-9851162-0-5

This book was professionally typeset on Reedsy. Find out more at reedsy.com

Contents

1

It can't be much further, she assured herself. The soles of Abigail's feet were screaming at her. She'd gotten turned around but she was on the right track now. At least, she was fairly certain she was. It had been an hours long trek in the dark through this dense thicket, led by nothing other than the light of her lantern. A cool breeze sent a chill down to her toes. She wrapped her duster around herself as tightly as she could. The cold had sprung up on her tonight but Abigail Lambert prayed she wouldn't have to endure it for much longer. The Eastwood train line she was hoping to find buried somewhere behind these trees was due to have a train roll over its rails any minute now and she needed to beat the iron beast there. She couldn't afford to mess this one up.

Not *again*.

The beauty of tonight's plan was in its simplicity. All it would demand of her was, ostensibly, to do absolutely nothing. The train would take care of everything; she just had to make sure she arrived early enough to meet it. Once she got to the tracks, she figured, there was almost nothing she could do to ruin this attempt as she'd done all the others. It wasn't that she couldn't go through with it; she'd seen every attempt through to its conclusion and somehow, she'd still managed to fail every time. Ropes that could wrangle the strongest mare would snap under the weight of her thrashing. Rifles that could shoot the scales off a snake from a hundred yards away would jam the moment they were aimed in her direction. She blamed herself in the aftermath of each attempt and by now, she'd simply lost count of how many times she'd even tried. It's not like that fact mattered much to her, not much did these days. She only needed to be successful once and tonight would be that night.

She arrived at a break in the tree line to discover the tracks. She laid her lantern down beside the tracks and laid down with her back to the planks. She stared at the night sky, filled with stars but seeing only the darkness between them, when it occurred to her that in this orientation, the train was liable to roll right over her and this entire trek would have been for naught. She laid herself perpendicular to the tracks, the frigid steel rail sending a shiver through her whole body when she laid her neck down upon it. She looked to her left, and then to her right, wondering if she wanted to face the train once it arrived.

It was to her right she spotted one of nature's curiosities: a lone flower, stalk standing tall as it stretched toward the sky. It grew out from beneath a crack in a pile of rocks just beside the tracks. Her attention drifted to the caterpillar as it slithered up the stalk. Just beyond it, she could see light from the train cutting through the trees up ahead. The rails tickled her from underneath, vibrating with the promise of her coming absolution.

The train sped forward as plumes of smoke billowed out into the night air. A sense of peace washed over her as she closed her eyes, the distance between her and the iron beast closing by the second. Everything she'd been forced to endure up to this point would soon be washed away and she could finally rest. She could finally confront God or fate or whatever force kept air in her lungs and blood pumping through her veins to demand answers for what she'd been forced to suffer in the fifteen years since she had to leave home and the downward spiral that ensued. That meeting though, much to her dismay, would be delayed.

The steam engine burst in a brilliant display of raging flames, its brakes crying the shrill scream of metal grinding on metal. The rails quaked beneath her. She prayed for anyone that might be listening to please let this be it, but it could not be so. The train ground to a halt mere inches from Abigail's body. The warmth of the flames pinched her cheeks and she opened her eyes.

Still here.

She sat up and witnessed the train, the metal that once shrouded the engine, curled and stretched like the petals of a flower, flames burning out from within. She refused to forgive herself for not picking a spot a few feet closer to where it ultimately stopped, but the more thought she gave it; the quicker she realized had she chosen a spot ten, twenty or even a hundred feet in either direction—the train would've ground to a halt inches from her just the same. Her problem was not the method; it was what motivated those methods in the first place. She found that most times she wanted something in life, it was only after she'd abandoned those desires that what she initially wanted finally arrived. There would be no way to cheat this, however—as her yearning for death was likely her deepest.

People poured out of the train to see what had brought their late night journey to a sudden stop. It was then that Abigail grabbed her lantern and followed the tracks further into the woods and deeper into the darkness. About a half a mile down the tracks, she came upon a deserted train station.

She spotted a Stranger, dressed in his Sunday best and a top hat, sitting by his lonesome on a bench.

"Whoever you're waiting for is liable to be delayed," she told him.

"I sincerely doubt it!" He replied.

"Train's engine blew about half a mile up the tracks."

"Is everyone alright?"

"Can't say I stopped to check." Abigail stepped up onto the platform.

"Something troubling you?"

"I'm beginning to think I may be cursed to this life for the rest of eternity."

"Do you talk to most strangers this way?"

She thought it over. For whatever reason, she felt an odd sense of comfort and familiarity around him, like he'd been with her for longer than she might've ever realized.

"No, I suppose I don't."

"You know, some people might be inclined to call a life eternal a blessing."

"I ain't some people."

"Then who are you?"

"Just a woman who's ready to die."

"Ready to die?" He scoffed at the suggestion. "Nonsense! You have so much life ahead of you. God will call upon you when it's your time and not a moment sooner."

"I'd be hard pressed to believe a world as full of pain and suffering such as this would have someone looking after it."

"How can you deny God's will when we live its consequences?"

"With what I've seen? Quite easily."

"Even if we cannot appreciate it immediately, there is always a reason to God's will." He said.

"Reason? For what reason must the raped divine from their suffering? What do the families of the unjustly murdered have to learn from what was taken from them? There is no such thing as reason in a universe as unreasonable as this one."

"To imply a lack of reason is to imply a lack of God."

"I ain't implying."

"You don't believe God is watching over you?" He asked.

"He very well may be. But if all he does is watch, when so many could be spared sorrow with his intervention, what's that say about God?"

The Stranger considered her question.

"Sorrow is an important emotion," he said, "as is its sister, suffering. You might even say suffering is the default mode of being. It's in choosing to face the cruelty of being that allows us to cultivate the strength to bear it. It's the only way God knew we would measure up to the task."

"If you're the type to believe light can be found in darkness."

"Wherever there is darkness, there is light to counter it. You just have to be willing to uncover it."

"If telling yourself this makes bearing life easier on you, then more power to you. But I've searched high and low for that light and I'm convinced it ain't nowhere to be found."

She stepped onto the edge of the platform, out toward what little of the forest she could see. The Stranger took to his feet and stood beside her.

"That's a hard place to be," he told her. "But if you accept God's mission, if you carry hope home, well I reckon light must be waiting for you at the end of that road."

"I hate to break it to you, but I don't think God has a mission for any of us."

"Then we agree to disagree."

"Seems so." She stepped off the platform and left the Stranger behind at the station. She crossed the tracks and wandered back into the trees.

2

Night had given way to day as light pierced in through the cover of trees overhead. Abigail continued to roam in search of her next opportunity to greet Death at its door. After spending so long wandering in search of an end that would never manifest, time had become an irrelevant structure. Each day had become colored by the same shade of gray, obscuring the difference between weeks and months and ultimately making it impossible to tell whether she'd been wandering for two weeks or two years. Either way, the only constant throughout it all was an overriding sense that she'd been alive too long and there was some force refusing to let her change that.

Every moment blood continued to course through her veins presented another opportunity to dwell on mistakes made, moments of opportunity missed and memories of better times long past. She typically found herself struck by the pang of yearning for a time that no longer was as waves of inadequacy and regret washed over her. Every so often, however, a familiar voice carried by a comforting breeze would whisk her away into the embrace of a warming memory. Back to a time before the world lost so much of its color. Today, this wind shared a name with her older brother, Benjamin.

~ o ~

"Here," he whispered to her as he handed her the rifle. Abigail was all of 12 years old when her brother decided to teach her how to handle a weapon. Pa and Benji always made it look so easy, but her arms dropped as soon as she got a grip on it.

"You know what Pa'll do when he finds out about this?" she asked him.

"Don't you worry about Pa." It wasn't out of turn for Benjamin to intervene when their father got carried away with his disciplining of Abigail, a process that often amounted to a belt whipping. He could take it, and if he had to accept a few extra lashings to spare her—he'd do so without a second thought.

Benjamin directed Abigail's attention to the deer, grazing on a bit of grass about a half a dozen yards ahead of them. "First thing's first—you've gotta have proper form. You don't want to rest that finger on the trig—" Abigail accidentally popped off a shot, frightening the deer as it scurried away.

"I'm sorry."

"Don't you worry, now." He took the lead as they picked up the trail and ventured deeper into the woods. Benjamin noticed a spider in the midst of repairing its web, and he pointed it out to her.

"Do you know what this means?"

She shook her head.

"She's been through here." They continued in that direction until they spotted the creature just up ahead. They stopped and, without a word, Benjamin signaled Abigail to raise her rifle. She did just that.

"You might wanna take a deep breath when lining up your shot. Try not to get too excited this time."

"I'll do my best," she said with a wry smile. She raised her weapon and filled her lungs before pulling the trigger. She clipped the deer, but it staggered away.

"God damn my aim!" She shouted and she proceeded to smack herself across the head. Benjamin was quick to grab her arm and stop her.

"That ain't no way to treat yourself."

"Sorry."

"Go on," he said as he let go of her arm.

"I'll just ruin it again." She couldn't look him in the eye.

"With that attitude, you certainly will." He picked

her chin up to meet her gaze. "Your only hope of getting any better rests on you keepin' to try, you hear?"

She nodded.

"Now finish what you started."

She took the lead and approached where the deer had just been standing. There they found splotches of blood on the dirt forming a crimson trail due east. They followed it for some time before they spotted the wounded deer once again. At least fifty yards away, it was a long shot for someone as green as Abigail but she rose her rifle to take aim regardless. Her brother lowered the rifle for her before she could line up her shot.

"What's the probl—" He quickly pressed a finger to her lips. With his other hand, he pointed to a bear cub to their left, much closer to them than the deer.

~ o ~

And with another soft breeze, Abigail found herself whisked away from her memory to her present, where a bear cub scratched its back on the bark of a nearby tree. Momma bear couldn't be far off which, to Abigail, meant another opportunity had presented itself. She approached the cub.

"Hey there, little one," she whispered. The cub made eye contact with her and quickly rounded behind the tree for cover. It cried out. She crouched down to its level. "It's okay," she said as she inched closer. "I ain't gonna hurt ya." The cub cried out once more and the roar of its mother boomed from behind. Abigail turned around to spot Momma Bear in all her fury, staring her down. The bear huffed with enough force to shake the fallen leaves beneath her. Abigail closed her eyes and threw up her arms as if to welcome the beast with a hug.

The bear charged straight at her, the distance between them closing with incredible speed. Abigail could feel the wind shift as the animal brought its mammoth paw up to strike, but just before it could knock Abigail to the ground, a gunshot echoed through the forest and Momma Bear slid to a dead stop at Abigail's feet. She opened her eyes, equal parts amazed and disappointed providence had once again intervened and spared her from death. The innards of the bear's recently vacated skull coated Abigail's boots. She looked up from the gory sight to the Good Samaritan on horseback who saved her life.

"Are you trying to get yourself killed?"

"As a matter of fact, I am." She shook the chunks of brain off her boots.

"You have a funny way of saying thank you, Miss."

"I wasn't trying to."

"To hell with you, then." He packed up his rifle and continued riding on. Abigail looked down at the body of the bear, the cub whining as it nuzzled its mother's lifeless corpse.

She wandered further south and happened upon the town of Valentine, a sleepy little outpost that was all that remained of a once boom town whose best days were firmly behind it. Just off the main street one would find a path to the silver mine that was once Valentine's central draw. When the prospect of silver dried up however, most folk took that as a sign to move on. For those that remained, a couple of families and handful of folks that traded with the occasional passersby, Valentine was now a perfect spot for those who preferred quiet over the excitement of new folks pouring in looking to stake their claim.

Abigail travelled up the main street with its general store, undertaker and pelt trader to one side. A blacksmith kept shop across the street beside the sheriff's station. At the end of the road, she spotted what became Valentine's crown jewel after the silver dried up: Jackson's Saloon.

She entered to see a handful of patrons scattered about at the tables. Most drinking by their lonesome, the laughter of a trio of rabble-rousers bounced up and down the walls of the place. Inconsistent with the sleepier quality of the rest of the patrons, their conversation which was liable to be heard all the way down the street was proof enough that they'd drifted into Valentine from elsewhere; much the same as Abigail. She paid them no mind, despite how difficult they were making such a task, and approached the bar.

"Whaddaya got?" She asked the bartender.

"Here," he turned to the wall of bottles behind him and placed a bottle of Payne Whiskey on the bar. "We serve whiskey." He placed an empty glass in front of her.

"You got anything that actually tastes good?"

"You're aware this is a bar, right miss?"

"I can give you something you'll like the taste of, honey!" The rabble-rouser who reeked of alcohol even from three yards away stood up from the table and gyrated his hips in her direction. Whatever hope of avoiding a confrontation Abigail had beforehand was now dashed. She turned toward him and he waltzed over to her, leaving his buddies behind back at the table.

"I'll pass," she said.

"What's the matter? Don't think you can handle all this?" As he leaned on the bar beside her, the combination of alcohol and cigarettes on his breath was enough to singe the hairs in Abigail's nostrils.

"Are you sure *you* can handle all this?"

"What's it take to get in with you, missy?" He furled his brow.

"You're very persistent."

"Momma didn't raise no quitter!" He smacked the bar with his fist.

"Tell ya what," she whispered to him. "Since you're so eager to whip out that pistol of yours, just do it right here in front of everybody. I'm sure everyone could use the laugh." Abigail's suitor, flummoxed, looked around the bar as everyone (including his buddies) hooted and hollered. The smile melted off his face to reveal the scowl beneath.

"You think you're funny, don'tcha bitch?"

"I have my moments."

"Do you know who you're talking to? Me and my boys are wanted in three different states!"

"Orville!" one of his cronies shouted from across the saloon. "Why you gotta go yelling that everywhere we go!"

"Well," she informed Orville, "you ain't wanted here. So beat it." She turned her attention back to her glass.

"Someone ought to teach you some manners!"

He slammed his hand onto her shoulder, but Abigail was quick on the draw. She shot him twice in the gut and quickly whipped around toward his buddies at the other end of the saloon. They sprang to their feet and managed to grab a hold of their pistols but not before Abigail gunned them both down. The whole bar sat stunned to silence by the sight. As Abigail towered over Orville's body, bleeding out onto the floor, she was struck by inspiration.

"Who wants to go get the sheriff?" Abigail petitioned. No one dared move an inch. She turned toward the bartender, gun still in hand. "Seems like it's you." She crossed over behind the bar. "Go on!" She commanded, waving him off like a dog. Jackson ran out of his business. She grabbed the whiskey she'd yet to try and took a swig straight from the bottle. "That ain't half bad." It wasn't but a few moments until Sheriff Weston entered the saloon armed with his rifle, to find Abigail behind the bar.

"You must be the sheriff!" She said.

"When you told me a little lady was causing all this ruckus, I thought you was joking," he said to the barkeep.

"Ain't no jokers here, sheriff. Except the dead ones on the floor." She said.

"I see," he said, looking over the carnage. "Now, why you gotta come into my town and start trouble? Scare all these nice folk?"

"I didn't come here to kill the first person that crossed me, if that's what you're implying."

"I ain't implying nothing. But mixing drifters is a recipe for disaster and I don't take too kindly to you wandering into my town, thinking you've got the right to take a man's life. Let alone three."

"Whaddaya gonna do about it, sheriff?"

"You wanna try that again?" His grip on the rifle tightened.

"What's it take to get hanged in this town?"

"Toss your weapon and I'll see to it that doesn't happen, ma'am."

"That doesn't answer my question."

"Are you askin' to be hanged?"

"Only cause I deserve it."

"Can't say I've ever heard of someone bargaining for their own execution."

"I want your word, sheriff."

"On what?"

"If I surrender myself into your custody, I will be hanged."

"Ma'am, at this point, you don't have much a choice in the matter."

"Can I have your word?" The air between them was thick with the silence.

"Ain't no one gonna cheat the hangman in my town. Not if they's earned it."

"That's all I wanted to hear." Abigail holstered her gun and approached the sheriff with her wrists out, ready for what awaited her.

The Sheriff wasted no time in carting her out to the gallows out behind the sheriff's station. The whole town had gathered to witness the hanging. As the executioner wrapped the noose around her neck, Abigail couldn't help but smile as the rope squeezed around her neck. *This time*, she thought, *it would work*. A wave of peace washed over her as she could feel one foot in this life and another in the next. The citizens of Valentine took her look of serenity as the consequence of wanton bloodlust. One woman even covered her young son's eyes from the horror, but however the town felt would be of no mind to Abigail in a few short moments.

The executioner, one of the town's folk eager to jump at the opportunity, approached the lever. All was quiet. He made eye contact with the Sheriff, who nodded. He pulled the lever and down a short drop Abigail went. She thrashed for no longer than a second before the rope snapped and she fell down onto the dirt. The crowd gasped! Abigail couldn't help but laugh at her naivety for thinking that this time it would work. As her laughter grew louder and more unhinged, the crowd could barely contain themselves. The sheriff stomped over to Abigail as she continued to laugh.

"Do it, Sheriff!" She commanded. "Don't hesitate!"

He pulled out his pistol and aimed square at her head. At this distance, there's no way he could miss. She looked him in the eye as he did it, but when he pulled the trigger, the gun backfired—sending the chamber flying out of the gun and into the crowd, destroying the revolver.

"What in the hell?" He'd never seen anything like it. The sight inspired only more laughter from Abigail, and by now the crowd was in uproar, approaching the gallows to finish themselves what the Sheriff couldn't.

"Get her out of here!" He shouted at the executioner. He climbed down to Abigail and dragged her out from beneath the gallows. The Sheriff climbed down to help as the crowd closed in. They picked a hysterical Abigail up off the ground and dragged her into the Sheriff's station, shutting the door behind them.

3

Abigail, age 13, laid on her belly upon the floor of the bedroom she shared with her brother. In front of her rested a canvas, with a few cups of different color paints beside her. As her brush glided up, down and around the canvas, the portrait of a butterfly in blue was beginning to take shape. It was then that her father, Roscoe, entered the room.

"Abigail?"

"Yes, Daddy?" She continued to paint, her gaze locked to the painting.

"Where's your brother?"

"I remember him saying someth—"

"Look at me when I'm speaking to you." He said. She turned to him.

"He said he was working in the barn."

"What's this supposed to be?" He asked as he stepped closer to get a better look at her artwork. She sat up on the floor and held up the canvas.

"It's a butterfly!"

"That ain't like no butterfly I ever saw."

"What's it look like to you, then?"

"Like it needs a lot of work."

Abigail bit her lip.

"Where'd you get all this?"

"Momma picked up this canvas and some paints for me last time she was in town."

"Momma paid for this?"

"Yes?"

Roscoe ripped the canvas off the floor and stormed out of the room. "Caroline!"

"Daddy!" Abigail chased after him. Downstairs, Roscoe stomped into the cramped kitchen where his wife, Caroline, cut vegetables for the evening supper.

"Just what in the hell were you thinking with this?"

"No, no." She shook her head. "You ain't gonna come in here barking at me like that."

"What inspired you to waste our money on this kinda frivolity?" He threw the canvas at her feet. Abigail hid behind the wall at the foot of the stairs, listening in to the argument. "There ain't enough work around here to keep her busy?"

"Life ain't all about work, Roscoe!" she said. " She's just a child!"

"She ain't much younger than you were when we got married."

She dropped the knife on the counter and turned

to him. "What's it to ya? Honestly?"

"It's a waste of my goddamn money." He said.

"It's not a waste of money!" Abigail shouted. She looked her father in the eye. "It's a butterfly!" She wasted no time in stomping across the kitchen and out of the house. She crossed the yard, over to the clothesline and quietly sniffled to herself. The blankets and dresses swayed in the wind around her. She stared off into the distance, at the leaves of the trees as they blew with the breeze. Hiding behind the trunks, she spotted something suspect.

Something moved just behind the tree line. Could it have been a deer? The shadow's shape seemed strange for a deer, and as she followed the path of the shifting shadow it became apparent that there was more than one of whatever was hiding in the woods.

An arrow arced downward from the sky, tearing a hole through a blanket on the clothesline before piercing the dirt. She looked down upon the arrow when another came down. Followed by another and another. Her eyes met the treeline once again, only to spot a tribe of Natives as they began to swoop in. Abigail burst back inside the house.

"Momma! Injuns!" Abigail cried. Caroline peered out the window at the coming wave. Roscoe shouted for Benjamin as he ran to the bedroom to retrieve his rifle.

"What are we gonna do, Momma?"

"Whatever we have to, sweetheart." She held her daughter close, attempting to assure her with her embrace even if unassured herself.

Roscoe and Benjamin entered the living room with their rifles in hand. A rock crashed in through one of the windows. Abigail yelled and clutched tighter onto her mother's dress. Roscoe cleared the broken glass out by wiping his rifle along the window frame. Cleared of debris, he started firing in the direction of every native he could see.

"Take that you savage sons of bitches!"

"Momma!" Benjamin shouted. "Get away from the windows!"

"How many of them are there, Roscoe?" Caroline asked.

"Hard to tell." He popped off another shot, taking one of them down mid-stride. Roscoe tried to get a count on them, but for every one of them he gunned down, it seemed as though two more sprouted from behind the trees to replace them. The farm was being swarmed, and it would take nothing short of a miracle for the Lamberts to repel the invading force.

Another rock came flying in through a window on the opposite side of the house. Benjamin crossed over and took cover beside the window. Every time he popped his head out from cover, the Natives were flinging everything they had in his direction. No matter how hard he tried, he couldn't get a clear shot on them. Not until they'd disappeared out of view of the window, along the sides of the house. When he brought up his rifle to see, one of them emerged from beneath the window frame and grabbed Benjamin.

"Roscoe!" Caroline shouted. He whipped around with his gun, but another native emerged from behind Roscoe and grabbed him through the window, much the same as his son. He held on tight to his rifle, barring himself against the window with the weapon. It was the only thing keeping him from being dragged outside to suffer the wrath of the Native at his throat. Roscoe's vision began to go dark as the grip around his neck tightened. He reached for his pistol, but dropped it on the floor.

"Caroline!" He screeched out with strained breath. He kicked the gun over to her. She took it in hand and aimed at the Native attacking her son. She took her shot and Abigail screamed. Her son's attacker flew backward from the shot to the head, and Benjamin collapsed to the ground, gasping for air.

"Take your sister upstairs!" She yelled. Benjamin crawled over to them.

"We've gotta go, Abby!" Abigail clutched her mother tighter. Benjamin grabbed her by the arm and ripped her off of her mother, dragging her up the stairs. The Native strangling Roscoe wrapped his arm around his neck, freeing up a hand so he could unsheathe the knife at his waist. Caroline aimed now at her husband's attacker, but an arrow flew in through the window behind her—striking her through the back of the skull and springing her eye out its socket.

"Momma!" Abigail screamed as she watched her mother fall to the ground. She wrangled her way out of her brother's grasp and crawled back down the stairs toward her mother's body. Blood pooled beneath her, staining Abigail's dress. The crack of Roscoe's neck rung out over the commotion, and he was dragged out of the window he'd been clinging to so tightly. As Abigail took her mother's pistol in hand, Benjamin scooped her up from behind and the Natives poured in from both sides of the house. The remaining Lamberts retreated upstairs and Benjamin barred the door shut by knocking over an armoire.

The sounds of the invaders scurrying beneath them like rats sent vibrations up through the wooden planks of the house. Benjamin and Abigail pushed themselves up against the wall by a window opposite the door. The chanting of the Natives summiting the stairs grew louder as they held each other tighter. It wasn't long after that they started to break down the door, it could be seconds before they broke the meager defenses. Benjamin looked out the window behind them.

"Come on." He opened the window and they climbed out onto the veranda. "I'll lower you down," he told her.

"What about you?"

"I can take the drop." He took the gun from her hands and threw it on the ground. They were only a single story off the ground, but as she looked down at the drop, you might as well have been asking her to hop off a cliff.

"I can't." She cried.

"Yes you can."

"What if—" He cut her off before she had the chance to talk herself out of it.

"There ain't no time for if's, Abby!" She climbed down onto the ledge and Benjamin laid down on his belly, taking her arms in both hands and lowering her as far as he could reach. "I'm gonna let go now, okay?" She shook her head. "You're gonna be fine." He dropped her and she fell no more than two or three feet to the ground. As she stood up, she could hear the Natives crashing through the door upstairs, and a pair of them poured out of the window and grabbed Benjamin. She grabbed the pistol off the ground and took aim.

"Run!" He shouted at her.

"I can't leave you!" She took a shot, but it flew past the heads of her brother's attackers.

"You've gotta run, Abby!" He shouted as he struggled to keep the Natives off him. "Run and don't look back!" They lifted him off the veranda and dragged him back inside.

She couldn't see clearly through the tears that welled up in her eyes. She did as her brother demanded and ran. The Natives, too busy storming the house, did not notice her as she fled. She flew as quickly as her legs would carry her, but she stopped in her tracks when a Native boy emerged from behind a tree, bow and arrow at the ready. She drew her gun and for the moment, it was a standoff. They stood there as the seconds stretched out their anxiety over who would take the first shot.

Abigail's arm grew heavy and she lowered her weapon. The Native boy lined up his shot, and she closed her eyes, ready for whatever he planned to do to her. In a single moment, every horror story her father recanted to her of Natives on the frontier scalping and dismembering men like her father and her brother. Roscoe had spared her the details of what tribes often did with the women they found on their raids, but she could only imagine it was a fate as bad, if not worse, than death. She felt the wind carry the arrow as he released it, and it flew past her ear and landed in the tree behind her. She gasped and opened her eyes. He crossed over to the tree and turned to look at her. She looked back at him. He took the arrow out of the tree and headed toward the farm.

Abigail continued to run. She cut her legs on fallen branches, leaving little splotches of blood in her wake like wounded prey. Rain poured down as she reached a creek with a raging current. She waded through the water, nearly losing her balance but making it over to the other side. She continued to run, as fast as she could until her lungs could barely keep any air at all within them. She collapsed to her knees.

The tears flowed freely, the moment's respite bringing her adrenaline down and spiking her sense of isolation. She heard the snap of twigs nearby and quickly raised her gun.

"Who goes there!" She looked around and from behind the trees, a man no more than four years her senior dressed all in black save for the red bandana around his neck, emerged with his hands up.

"I mean you no harm, little missy." He approached her and extended a hand. "What's your name?"

"Abigail." She kept her gun on him.

"Pleasure to meet you, Abigail. My name's Sid."

~ o ~

Abigail awoke with a gasp on the bench inside

this Valentine jail cell. She rubbed the bruises on her neck, still sore from the failed hanging the day before. How could she have been so naïve as to think that her escape would be granted at someone else's hand? In hindsight she should've seen how this plan would get botched like all the others, but ruminating on her failures as she often did always brought similar conclusions. If there's anything she should've learned by now it's if you want to get something done right, you've gotta do it yourself. Now, if only she could get the *right* part down…

The door to the sheriff's station opened and Abigail could hear a conversation in progress.

"Are they gonna have to come knocking on our doors before you do something about them?" She overheard a strange yet familiar voice say.

"My hands are tied, Jeb." The other voice was that of the Sheriff's. "I could deputize every man in this town and it'd still be a suicide mission." Abigail's ears perked up. She sat upright in her cell.

"So you're just gonna let them have their run of the place?" Jeb asked.

"What would you have me do?" The Sheriff asked in reply. Jeb crossed the tiny sheriff's station into Abigail's view and mulled over what he might have to do himself since the Sheriff was proving useless. He turned his attention toward her and they instantly recognized each other.

"Makin' friends, I see." Jeb remarked. The Sheriff leaned into Abigail's field of view.

"You two know each other?" The Sheriff asked him.

"I saved her from a bear a few days ago," he explained. "She was none too thankful after the fact."

"Perhaps you wasted the bullet," said the Sheriff.

"That's what I'd meant to tell ya." Abigail replied. Jeb shook his head.

"If you're not gonna do something about 'em, then I'll have to." Jeb told him.

"You're gonna get yourself killed." He warned him.

"Then let me do it!" Abigail suggested.

"You even know what we're talking about?" Jeb asked her.

"No, but if it would kill you then maybe it'll get done for me what the Sheriff failed to." She said.

"You watch your tongue, girl." The Sheriff said, mulling it over. Jeb could see him play out the scenario in his head.

"Don't tell me you're entertaining this ridiculousness." He asked the Sheriff.

"From what I saw yesterday, it would seem providence is on her side." He replied.

"That ain't no strategy I ever heard of." Jeb said.

"Have some faith, Jeb!" Abigail said.

"That's rich." He grumbled.

"Would anyone like to inform me as to what has him so scared of action?" She asked as she pointed at the sheriff.

"A gang of outlaws has moved into Nigel Dicken's farm." Jeb said.

"And I assume Nigel ain't too pleased?" She asked.

"They shot him dead." The Sheriff said.

"Trouble is there's twenty, maybe twenty five of them holed up there by my count." Jeb said.

"Sounds fun." Abigail said.

"You think you're gonna take them all out?" The Sheriff asked her.

"All of 'em? Probably not. But I'll die trying which, it would seem, works out for the both of us." She said.

"So we send her up there, she gets killed, pisses them off, and then we get their wrath sent down upon us." Jeb explained. "That sound like a plan to you?" He asked the Sheriff. He said nothing as he opened Abigail's cell and tied her wrists together with a rope. He led her out of the station and up onto the back of a horse out front.

"Don't tell me you're serious!" He pleaded.

"You wanted me to do something. This is something." The Sheriff unhitched the horse and mounted up onto the same steed Abigail sat atop. "You ready?" He asked Abigail.

"Not like I have much of a choice."

The Sheriff belted out a hearty laugh and they rode out for the Dicken's.

4

Less than a mile east of Valentine, the pair of them arrived just after nightfall, at the wooden gate of the sprawling ranch—the house overlooking them both from atop the hill. It would be a long walk to the house from here, and it was here that the Sheriff cut Abigail loose and lowered her off the horse.

"My gun?" She held out an open palm. He unholstered the gun she was arrested with, the very same gun she'd been carrying since she was forced to run from her homestead all those years ago. He held it out in front of her, but pulled back when she went to grab it. He unlocked the chamber and pocketed the remaining bullets. It was only then that he handed her the gun.

"What am I supposed to do with an empty gun?"

"Suicide mission, right?" The Sheriff tipped his hat to her and rode off back toward town. She holstered her gun and walked the main path toward the house. As she approached, she could just barely make out the men scattered about the property. A couple of them sat on the porch, feet kicked up like they owned the place. Over by the barn, a pair of them exited and approached the house. On the second story, she spotted another with his head poking out, staring her down. He whistled as soon as he could tell a woman was approaching, and the rest of the men followed suit, raising all kinds of ruckus upon her arrival.

"What have we got here?" One of them shouted.

"Oooh, momma! Hello, hello!" said another. The more 'gentlemanly' of the outlaws stepped off the porch and crossed over to her.

"Good evening, darling." He took her hand and gave it a kiss.

"So cordial," Abigail said.

"What brings someone as fine as yourself up around these parts?" He asked her. Even with her suitor at arm's length, the air was thick with the lust of every outlaw that surrounded her, undressing her with their eyes.

"I was told there was a gang of men holed up out here." She said, looking around. She locked eyes with her 'gentleman' suitor. "Can't say I see any *men* though." Every outlaw in earshot started hootin' and hollerin'.

"Well ain't you a little firecracker?" The outlaw asked her. Abigail leaned in close to him.

"You wanna watch me pop?" She whispered.

"What'd you have in mind?"

She swiped the gun out of his holster and shot him in the stomach! He cried out and keeled over, but she caught him in her grasp and used him as a human shield as the rest of the gang drew their weapons to return fire. She plowed forward, gunning down the outlaws with precision and fury—as if it was expressly what she'd been built to do. She made it to the front of the house, dropping her meat shield and kicking down the door.

Once inside, a pair of outlaws poured in on her left from the living room. She shot them both. Outlaws came in from the room opposite her and she took cover behind a wall. As they made their approach, she popped out from behind the wall to shoot them dead. Upstairs, a pair of them ran down the hall to the stairs but she shot one before he had the chance to make it down. He fell over the railing, landing on an oil lamp below. It wasn't long before the flames consumed his body and began to spread throughout the house.

She re-entered the foyer as the second outlaw, sporting a rifle, rushed down the stairs. She took her shot and emptied the contents of his skull on the steps behind him. He fell backward, his corpse riding the bloody stairway to hell all the way to the bottom. She approached the body on the stairs and took the rifle for herself. As the fires climbed up the walls to the second floor, screams echoed through the house. The pitch was too high to be that of any man, it must've been a woman's, maybe even a child's. The adrenaline pumping through Abigail's veins was enough to dull her hearing to such a thing as she continued her march up the steps.

Out of one of the rooms upstairs emerged an outlaw, which she quickly turned to and shot in the head, painting the wall behind him with what remained of his brains. Another outlaw emerged from a door behind her and choked her with his rifle. Further down the hallway, another one of the outlaws ran toward her, firing in her direction the whole way. She'd managed to turn around the one strangling her, filling his back full of his friend's bullets. She looked down at her attacker's boot and noticed a knife sticking out of it. As he lost his grip on both Abigail and his life, she slipped out of his grasp, took the knife from his boot and flung it at the other outlaw—the blade finding a new sheath within the outlaw's skull.

It appeared the assault was over. She crossed over to the outlaw she'd stuck with the knife and removed it from his skull. She wiped the blood off the blade with his own shirt. She walked down the hall to the room he'd emerged from as smoke filled the house behind her. She raised her rifle, kicked down the door and burst inside to an unexpected sight.

She spotted a young Mexican girl, not a day over 13, with her wrists and ankles tied to the bedpost. Her clothes were tattered, and it was anyone's guess how long they'd left her tied up here. The young girl couldn't take her eyes off Abigail's gun. She lowered the weapon and took the knife in hand as she approached the bed. The girl thrashed but the bonds that imprisoned her refused to break. Abigail stood over her and cut her free. The girl crawled across the bed and took cover behind the side opposite Abigail. She approached the girl and she scurried away toward the wall.

"Stay close to me." Abigail put away her knife and extended a hand. The young girl nodded and took her hand as she lifted herself off the ground. They left the bedroom, retreating back into the house which was now filled with smoke too thick to see through. They hugged the side wall as its opposite was now engulfed in flames. They ran out down the stairs and out of the burning house, having narrowly escaped before a wooden beam came crashing down onto the porch. Smoke and flames billowed out the broken windows as the girls coughed up a storm.

A surviving outlaw managed to spring out of the

house with his gun drawn and he fired at Abigail. She quickly returned fire with a shot to his leg, and he dropped to the floor. He yelled in pain and brought his gun up again but she shot it out of his hand.

"You can't take the girl!" He yelled through gritted teeth.

"You ain't really in a position to be making demands." Abigail said as she towered above him.

"I'm warning ya. If you take her, Colin will hunt you down to the ends of this Earth."

Without a second thought, she lifted her gun and shot him in the head. Abigail holstered her pistol and walked away from the property as it burned to the ground. She crossed the young girl who stood frozen in shock. She stared at the flames eating away at the wood in all their rage. She grabbed some nearby rocks off the ground and yelled as she flung them at the house. After she'd had enough, she turned toward Abigail, who was already halfway down the hill.

"Where are you going?" she shouted at her.

"Not sure yet," Abigail replied. "Thinking I might try walking off a cliff and seeing if I grow wings."

"Wait, you can't leave me!"

"Can't?"

"Don't you understand?" She asked as she'd finally caught up to Abigail, planting her feet in the ground to stop her in her tracks. "God has brought us together for a reason." Abigail couldn't help but laugh.

"Oh, you sweet girl." She kept walking.

"I prayed every night for God to save me from these animals. To take me back home!" She explained as she trailed behind Abigail. "And just when I was beginning to think he wasn't listening, you arrived!" It struck Abigail that there was an oddly Scottish underpinning to the way the girl spoke, betraying her dark skinned exterior.

"Well, if it was God's plan for me to save you, consider yourself saved."

"But that's only half of it. You need to help me get home."

"And where's home?"

"Just outside of Memphis."

"Tennessee! That's at least two thousand miles from here."

"So you understand why I can't do it alone."

"That maybe so, but I'll pass."

"You can't pass on God!" She shouted. Abigail turned on a dime to face her.

"God passed on me, girl! The sooner you learn there's no one looking out for you, the easier it'll be to take life *fucking* you in the way it has already and the ways it has yet to. Now, truly, I wish you well." Abigail turned and walked away. The girl stood there, flummoxed. She grabbed a rock and chucked it at Abigail, but she missed. She tried again and fell to the ground from the weight she'd put behind the throw. This one managed to hit Abigail, scraping her cheek. She put a finger to the wound and saw red. The first time she'd seen such a thing since she'd started wandering all those years ago.

"On your feet, girl," she commanded. The young girl stood. Abigail pointed at her to approach, and she did just that. "Clean your face up." The young girl wiped the dirt and soot from her cheeks on her clothes. Abigail looked into her eyes and saw the shades of memories she'd hoped to forget. "Do you have a name?"

"Esperanza."

~ o ~

That night in Valentine, the Sheriff snoozed in his chair with his feet kicked up on his desk. His slumber was interrupted when the door was kicked down off its hinges.

"Sweet Jesus!" He nearly fell off his chair from the scare. Two outlaws with bandanas over their faces entered with guns drawn and trained on the Sheriff. "Just who in the hell do you think you are?" He shouted as he stood up. In through the doorway entered Colin McCalister, clad in black with a thick mustache and a red bandana around his neck.

"I'm guessing you're the ring leader, here?" The Sheriff asked him. Colin huffed and punched him square in the jaw. He dropped like a rock onto the floor. Colin stepped over to him and placed a boot on his head. He winced in pain as Colin leaned down toward him.

"Where is the nearest train to Tennessee?"

"Ain't but a couple miles!" The Sheriff said, doing his best to cloak the quaking in his voice. "Follow the road due east and you'll come upon the station, sure enough." His attempt to hide it wasn't working out too well.

"Thank you, Sheriff." Colin lifted his boot off the man's head, and the Sheriff took a sigh of relief. He turned onto his back, only to spot Colin pointing a gun at him.

"Wait!" The Sheriff shouted as he brought his hands up to cover his face, but Colin shot him dead. The three of them exited the sheriff's station to find what remained of Colin's gang, about six other members, atop their horses.

"Wesley!" Colin called. He approached Wesley who mumbled to himself as he counted a deck of cards atop his horse. "Clean ya ears, boy!" Colin shouted as Wesley put away the deck.

"Sorry, Colin."

"I want you to meet us in Ridgewood."

"What about the train?" Colin approached him.

"Have I ever led you astray?"

"Colin, I was just askin—" Colin cut him off.

"Answer the question!" He boomed.

"No."

"Then get moving." Wesley did just that as Colin crossed over to his horse. "The rest of ya'll! We've got a train to catch."

~ ○ ~

Abigail and Esperanza sat in their seats aboard the train cart as it chugged along down the tracks. There were a handful of other riders on the train tonight, but everyone kept to themselves. Esperanza stared out the window at the dark scenery as it flew past.

"How long do you think it'll be?"

"As long as it takes." Abigail leaned back in her chair, tipped her hat over her eyes and did her best to get some shuteye. Struck by restlessness, Esperanza climbed over Abigail and wandered down the train cart. They'd barely managed to catch the last train before it left the station, and most everyone aboard was either keeping to themselves or took the opportunity to catch up on some rest before arriving at their next destination. They wouldn't sleep long however; the train's brakes screamed into the night and Esperanza fell to the floor as it ground to a halt. She got up and looked out the window. She spotted a handful of men with

42

lanterns approaching the train. It was hard to tell but it seemed like they were wearing bandanas across their faces. She rushed over to Abigail and shook her awake.

"What's going on?" She asked in a daze.

"We're being boarded." Esperanza said.

"By who?" Esperanza shrugged. She looked over to her side, to the train car closest the engine, and through the window she spotted Colin in the next car.

"We need to get off the train."

"What for?"

"Cause they're here for me." That was enough for Abigail to hop out of her seat. The two of them ducked into the next car. Just as they slid the door shut behind them, Colin and his gang entered.

"Good evening, ladies and gentlemen! I am so sorry to delay your journey this evening, but there is someone aboard this train that is very special to me, and it is my duty to find her." He announced. As he looked around, his gaze passed the window into the next cart, where he saw Abigail and Esperanza moving into the next cart over. "Much obliged!" He said as he tipped his hat and stomped forward to give chase.

Abigail and Esperanza left another cabin car behind them and found themselves in one meant for storage. Abigail closed the door behind them as Esperanza crossed over to a nearby crate.

"Help me move this." The two of them pushed the crate in front of the door. Two men smoking cigarillos stared at them as they did it, bemused, a sight far more interesting than the card game the girls had just interrupted.

"Excuse us, gentlemen." Abigail said as they crossed the cart to the other side. Gunshots blew holes through the door behind them, and Colin began ripping boards off the door to get a look inside.

"Esperanza!" He shouted as he continued to rip through the door with his brute strength. The two girls exited the cart and found themselves at the end of the train. Abigail barred the door shut with its metal bar.

"What now?" Esperanza asked.

"We run." And run they did, off the train and into the trees.

Gunshots rang out as Colin shot his way through the door and managed to squeeze an arm out through the planks, lifting the metal bar and swinging open the door. He stormed out of the cart, the rest of his gang behind him.

"Search the area, they can't have gone far!" He commanded. Far they were not, but they ran as fast as they could.

"Don't stop!" Abigail said. They ran until they

could barely manage it any longer, every gasp for air like knives in their lungs and blood like broken glass pumping through their veins. With the gang out of earshot and enough distance between them and the train, they stopped to catch their breath.

"What do we do now?" Esperanza asked.

"Stay off the train lines, for one." Abigail heaved. "Suppose we head for the nearest town."

"Where's that?"

"Ridgewood, I think." Abigail said as she sat down on the dirt.

"We're not going now?" She asked.

"It's the middle of the night and it's liable to take us a day or so on foot to get there but if your objective is to waste time walking in circles, then help yourself. I'll wait till dawn." Abigail said as she turned about on the ground in an effort to find some kind of comfortable position on the floor.

"What about Colin?"

"You're welcome to stay up all night and keep watch." She replied as she tipped her hat over her face. Esperanza did what she could to take her up on that, sitting with her back against a tree facing the direction they came from. At least, the direction she was pretty sure they came from—after all, it was the middle of the night and in the absence of light, darkness looked identical from all sides. The first couple of times her head grew heavy from weariness and dropped, she snapped back awake, but it wasn't long at all before she took Abigail's lead and dozed off herself.

5

The next morning, Esperanza awakened when she felt a forceful jolt to her leg. Her eyes shot open wide to identify the threat. She feared having attracted the attention of a hungry animal, or worse, being spotted by the animals they left behind on the train the night before but when she saw it was Abigail that'd kicked her awake, she quickly relaxed.

"Let's go." Abigail demanded, wasting no time at all as she started her march to Ridgewood, whether the girl was ready to join her or not. Esperanza took to her feet and followed Abigail in silence for some time until the quiet was broken by a faint whimper hidden within the trees.

"Do you hear that?" Esperanza asked. The closer they got to the sound, the clearer it became that there was a wounded *something* nearby. Esperanza suffered from a virulent case of a bleeding heart, and the prospect of a creature in trouble carried her like a wind over the small hill beyond them. There at its base, they spotted a dog with its leg caught in a bear trap.

"Poor thing!" She cried as she approached the dog. Abigail walked up behind her and drew her gun.

"What do you think you're doing?" Esperanza shouted.

"Putting it out of its misery?" Was it not obvious?

"We're not killing her!" Esperanza took a knee between Abigail's gun and the dog.

"It'd be crueler to leave it."

"We're not doing that either." Esperanza gripped the jaws of the trap with as much strength as she could muster, but no matter how hard she tried to force it apart, the tension was too strong.

"You're wasting your time, girl." Abigail's attempt at dissuasion proved fruitless as Esperanza refused to quit, rusty metal digging into her fingers as she tried to free the poor dog. "I'm just talking to myself, it seems," Abigail muttered under her breath.

"Are you gonna help me or not?" Abigail holstered her gun and took a knee beside the trap. She gripped the jaws and they managed to force it open enough for the dog to slip out and hobble away behind a nearby tree. Esperanza tried to soothe the creature, calling out to it. "It's okay, girl. Come here." She extended a hand, and the dog limped toward her. She gave it a pat on the head. "Good girl, Jules!" The dog barked and she laughed.

"Now you're naming the damn thing?"

"And?"

"I ain't wasting a second of my time trying to keep that thing fed."

"No one asked you to."

"So long's we understand each other." Abigail rose to her feet and continued onward.

"Come on, Jules!" Esperanza shouted at the dog, seemingly receptive to its new name. It limped along beside her as they continued through the woods.

The day melted away as they headed east for Ridgewood, finally arriving at the town as the sun was beginning to set. For most towns this far west of the Mississippi, Ridgewood was among one of the more affluent. A local connection to the railroad was mostly to thank for that, providing a healthy clip of people passing through and bringing their business. The town was attractive enough to even get some of those once travelers to become permanent residents, hoping to stake their claim to a piece of the town's potential economic spoils.

On this evening, Abigail, Esperanza and Jules would pass through its paved stone roads in search of a way to expedite their journey to Tennessee. As they walked down main street, Abigail did the one thing she did most often when she wandered into a new town: hit the saloon. This time, as opposed to a more typical blackout inebriation, she would instead be searching for information on tap. The three of them entered the saloon, a label hardly befitting of the place compared to the creaky watering hole Abigail found herself in back in Valentine.

The brick walls towered high, with ornate railing lining the second floor. Upstairs, this establishment played host to various tables at which one could partake in card games of chance. There were at least a dozen people playing at these tables, and that's just the ones they could see from the ground floor. If drinking was all you were after, then the first floor presented plenty of space for one to indulge in their chosen poison. Live piano echoed throughout from the back of the room, providing entertainment for those who needed an aural stimulant to mix with the alcohol. The three of them were taking in the sight as they entered, but they took not so much as a step before they were berated by the barkeep.

"She's gotta stay outside!" He yelled.

"That dog's cleaner than most of the people in here!" Abigail replied.

"The dog, too!" He shouted.

"Let's go, Jules." Esperanza said as she exited, the dog following suit. She took a seat on the curb and spoke to Jules directly. 'How's your leg, girl?"

The wound had begun to scab over, it wasn't deep enough to be fatal, but she was still hobbling around with a limp. "How'd you end up in that trap, huh?" She asked as she rubbed Jules all over. The dog barked. "Guess we all find ourselves trapped at one point or another." Abigail exited the saloon, and Esperanza stood as soon as she saw her.

"So?" Esperanza asked.

"Stable's this way." She pointed down the street to a wooden building that looked just about ready to be condemned. It was hard to believe a business of any kind ran out of there, and its state of disrepair stood out between the sturdier buildings and livelier businesses that were its neighbors. What they couldn't know was that the owner chose to spend most of his revenue on keeping pace with his taste for alcohol. So long as there wasn't a problem with the roof, he was content to keep contributing to the impending problem with his liver.

"This is the place?" Esperanza asked as they approached the building.

"That's what the man said." Abigail pushed open the double doors at the front and entered. "Hello?" No reply. Esperanza kept her distance and stayed outside by the door. Abigail looked around, but it was hard to make out much of anything with the little light let in from outside. She could just barely see three horses across the different pens, but no sign of human life. "Anybody here?" she called out. Out of the shadows behind her, emerged a cocked and loaded six shooter pointed at the back of Abigail's head.

"Is this how you greet all your prospective customers?" She asked.

"Only the ones that deserve it," a gravelly voice replied. There was something unmistakably familiar about his voice to Abigail, and she turned to find an answer to her suspicions.

"Bill Decker!" She shouted as she disregarded the loaded gun in her face. She pushed it to the side and gave him a hug.

"Get off me, woman!" He yelled, dumbfounded with her cavalier attitude toward having a gun pointed at her. He pushed her off. She pointed to his eye patch.

"That's new." She said.

"You know this man?" Esperanza took a few careful steps past the door, but still close enough to the exit to duck out in case things got hairy.

"We used to ride together." Abigail said.

"That was a *long* time ago." Bill holstered his gun. He crossed over to one of the horses. "How did you find me?"

"Not on purpose, that's for sure."

"Little Abigail Lambert stumbles back into my

life needing something from me. Glad to see *some* things never change." He said with a wry smile.

"Can't say the same for you. You finally got that stable you were after!"

"I don't know if this piece of shit's what I pictured—but it's something." He took some horse feed in hand and fed one of the horses.

"What would you charge me for two horses?" Abigail asked.

"For you? Nothing." He continued to the next horse.

"You'd give them to me for free?"

"You misunderstand." Bill clarified. "They'll cost you nothing, because I ain't selling you no horses."

"Why not?"

"Cause you wouldn't be able to afford what they cost."

"Try me."

"Five thousand dollars."

"That's ridiculous! There ain't no pair of horses on this Earth worth no five thousand dollars!"

"You're right. Cause it's five thousand *per.*"

"Ain't no wonder this place is falling to shit if that's what you're charging."

"It's what I'm charging *you.*" He said.

"Because I'm so special?"

"Because it's what you owe me."

"I owe you?" Would he really be so petty? Over

something so long ago?

"You promised me ten grand in that coffin, and there wadn't so much as a dime."

"That ain't my fault!" Abigail shouted. He threw the horse feed on the ground and stomped over to her.

"You're lucky I don't shoot you where you stand for leading me into that ambush!"

"I didn't know Sid was gonna follow us!"

"Don't give me that load of shit!"

"I'll just buy my horses elsewhere."

"Good luck with that darling. This may be the shittiest game in town, but it's also the only one."

"You'd really leave me hanging dry like this?" Abigail asked him.

"Like you left me holding the bag at Reedy Creek? It's cause of me you even made it out of there alive, you ingrate! I ain't so much as heard one thank you out your mouth since you got here!" Abigail stormed out of the stable. "Same old Abigail, always running from shit she started!"

"Fuck you, Bill!" Abigail stomped past Esperanza. "Let's go."

Esperanza looked back at Bill.

"You heard her, girl." He spit. "Git."

To her, the only thing more fascinating than how miserly this man behaved was the warmth with which Abigail greeted him. Esperanza was under the impression whatever faculty allowed Abigail to feel anything positive had long since broken down, but it was still in there, lying dormant and awaiting the right stimuli to awaken. The point being that beneath the tough exterior, there was an Abigail she'd yet to meet—one that Bill may or may not have known at one point in the past, and maybe, just maybe—there'd be an opportunity to meet her in the future.

"What do we do now?" Esperanza asked her.

"He can't be the only game in town," Abigail replied. She looked up the street to a general store and figured she could pop in for a potential lead. Much to her dismay, the shop keeper informed her Bill was, in fact, the only proprietor of horses in Ridgewood, and it would be some hundred miles to the next town if she intended on attempting to buy some there. She thanked him for his time and returned to the street.

"We're not walking a hundred miles on foot, are we?" Esperanza asked her.

"It's either that, or we wait for ten thousand dollars to fall from the sky."

"Where would we even find money like that?" Esperanza asked.

Abigail pondered the thought. It might be years of work to accumulate such a sum under any business in town. It was anyone's guess as to how long it would take Colin and his gang to roll into town before that ever happened, so she quickly abandoned the possibility. The most expedient way to make such a sum would also likely be the most dangerous, but time was not a currency they could afford to spend much of.

Abigail walked up the street, Esperanza and Jules behind her, to the sheriff station. What she sought wasn't out front so she crossed over to the side of the building and found the board there. Posted on the wall were more than a dozen wanted posters.

"Tell me what you see." Abigail asked her.

Esperanza scanned the board for the poster with the most zeroes, but after tallying the bounties across every poster she could see, it wouldn't be nearly enough for both horses.

"If we caught all of these guys," she explained, "and then it turned out each of them had a kid with separate bounties on their heads, we still wouldn't have enough for just one."

"Well that won't do at all." Abigail sighed. "Guess we're walking." As Abigail began the hundred mile journey, Esperanza stayed behind at the board; one poster buried beneath the others had caught her attention. She uncovered the handbill.

"Abigail!" She shouted.

Abigail stopped in her tracks and spotted Esperanza back at the board with the poster in hand. She returned to the board, and Esperanza handed it to her. There she saw a drawing of a man with a thick handlebar mustache, but that's about all she could divine from the poster. She shoved the poster into Esperanza's chest.

"Read it." Abigail commanded.

"Joseph Bacall and the Joseph Bacall gang, wanted for murder and stagecoach robbery." She scanned the rest of the handbill. "They're offering $2500 for Joseph and $300 for each member of his gang."

"What's that all together?" Abigail asked.

"About a hundred bucks short of five thousand."

"I suppose one horse is better than none."

"If you can talk him down. He seemed pretty firm on price."

"You leave that to me. Handbill say anything about where we might find Joseph and his gang?"

Esperanza scanned the handbill once again.

"Last known location," she said, "Pikes Basin."

6

They'd been travelling westward in the direction of Pike's Basin for some time when Esperanza's stomach grumbled. Abigail was long beyond the point of needing to keep up with regular meals—she'd go days without so much as a crumb more often than not, but hunger was a sensation she was rarely compelled to action by. The girl could not so easily tell her stomach to quiet down, as her last meal was well before she'd met Abigail's acquaintance.

The McCalister gang was a large one, at least, before Abigail crossed their path. While a few of them reveled in the vagrancy of the outlaw lifestyle, most of them were a patchwork of families who'd lost everything they'd ever worked towards for one reason or another and found both family and security under Colin's stead. While the men would ride out and bring back money by *any* means necessary, the women would stay back at wherever they'd made camp for now and prepare the group's meals. While it was far from a regal feast, Esperanza's mind was presently drowning in memories of Aunt Cass's stew. The growl of her stomach was underpinned by a vicious echo, where even Jules barked in solidarity.

"Me too." Esperanza's legs grew heavier with every step they marched forward.

"Quit lagging." Abigail commanded from up ahead.

"If I had some food, it might be easier for me to keep up."

"You're welcome to the berries in that bush over there that may or may not be poison," Abigail said as she pointed in its direction. "Or maybe that pile of rocks over there. They look tasty."

"Do you get a rise out of belittling people?" Esperanza asked.

"Do you get a rise out of complaining?" Abigail replied.

"Forgive me," Esperanza said, "not all of us are trying to die of starvation."

"That's harder than it seems." Abigail could just make out a black and white critter on the ground up ahead. She raised her fist, and everyone stopped moving.

"What?"

Abigail pointed at the skunk.

"You can't be serious."

"Are you hungry or are you not?"

Esperanza looked down at Jules. She whimpered, but whether she was agreeing with Esperanza's apprehension or merely expressing the torture of sitting still with her bum leg while every fiber of her being pushed her to chase down the critter was anyone's guess. Esperanza looked back up at Abigail.

"What do you expect me to do?" Esperanza asked her.

She'd wandered on her own for so long, she wasn't used to having so much noise follow in her wake. That it didn't even occur to this girl that she take an active role in securing her meal left Abigail without words. If it meant the girl would shut up, she'd take on the hunt herself. It would only be temporary, anyway. All she had to do was get her to Tennessee, and Abigail would have her peace.

Abigail took the rifle slung across her back and laid it against a nearby tree. She crept over toward the skunk, careful not to rustle up too much noise and scare it off. Once close enough to attack, she dived for the ground with her arms out to catch the critter but the skunk was quick on its feet. It scurried away and sprayed Abigail in the process. Esperanza couldn't help but laugh.

"I'm guessing they kept you tied up cause you weren't good for much else." Abigail said.

"I'm sorry." Esperanza covered the smirk on her face with her hand.

Abigail's cheeks stung with the stench of a thousand foul pricks. She tried to wipe as much of the spray off her face as she could, but it did more to spread the smell than to remove it.

"Here." Abigail grabbed the rifle and threw it at Esperanza.

"What do you want me to do with this?"

"Catch supper," Abigail replied. "Where's our heading?"

"West?" She squeaked.

"Was that a question?"

"West!" Esperanza took the lead, and they scoured the woods in search of their supper. They came upon a deer grazing by its lonesome, and Abigail held Esperanza back before she could get close enough to scare it off.

"Line up your shot." Abigail whispered.

"From here? I can't aim that far."

"It's a rifle, you'll be fine."

Esperanza raised her weapon and pointed it at the deer, still munching on grass. She pressed her cheek to the rifle to line up her sights.

"Not like that, you're gonna bust your cheek open." Abigail instructed.

"I've got it!" Esperanza pulled the rifle away from her. They stood there for some time with

Esperanza's finger hovering above the trigger, but she couldn't bring herself to take the shot.

"What the hell's the matter with you?"

"I can't kill it."

"You wanna eat, don't you?"

"I'll try my luck with the berries." Esperanza tried to slip away, but Abigail grabbed her by the collar.

"Take the shot."

Esperanza hesitantly brought the rifle back up to aim and her finger trembled over the trigger. Her stomach growled, loud enough to catch the deer's attention. It blew at her and Esperanza, now without a second to lose, took the shot. She hit the deer in its side, but the animal stayed on its feet and did its best to stagger away.

"Kill it!" Abigail demanded.

Esperanza raised her rifle to take the kill shot. It was moving slow enough that she might land it properly this time but just before she could pull the trigger, Bill Decker emerged from behind one of the trees.

"What smells like hammered shit?" He boomed, and both the girls shouted from the surprise—Esperanza accidentally squeezed the trigger. He approached Abigail and pinched his nose. "I said God damn!" Bill fanned the air, as if that would help.

"What the hell are you doing here?" Abigail asked.

"Someone told me you were after Joseph Bacall."
He replied.

"So?"

"I couldn't, in good conscience, let you get yourself killed."

"That might be easier said than done, Bill."

"You just cost us supper!" Esperanza shouted at
him as she beat on his chest. He grabbed her by the
wrist.

"Relax, little girl. I saw you clip that deer. It won't
be long before it bleeds out."

"Go home, Bill." Abigail said, cribbing the rifle
from Esperanza's hands.

"I didn't hike halfway through this God forsaken
forest to go back home empty handed."

"Wouldn't be the first poor choice you've made,
now would it?" Abigail walked away.

"If we don't do this together," he warned, "then
I'm afraid we're competing for the same bounty."

"Oh, is that a fact?" Abigail said.

"I'm tryin'a help you."

"We don't need your help." Abigail wouldn't even
look at him. "Come on, girl."

Esperanza followed suit.

"I ain't followin' you!" Bill did exactly the opposite. "We're just headed in the same direction."

"Oh, cut the crap!" Abigail shouted.

They all heard the strained whine of the creature

up ahead. They found Esperanza's wounded deer laying on the ground, bleeding out from its wound. Abigail and Esperanza approached it, and Abigail drew a knife from her boot. She handed it to her.

"Finish what you started." Abigail told her.

Esperanza took to her knees beside the deer and held the knife to the animal's throat. Her hands trembled as she stared into its eye.

"The longer you wait, the more it'll suffer." Abigail told her. Jules whimpered.

Esperanza pressed the tip of the knife to the deer's throat, but she didn't have the strength to go through with it. Bill stomped over to her, took the knife and finished the deer off himself.

"What the hell are you doing?" Abigail shouted.

"You said it yourself, no point in making the thing suffer!" He said.

"That ain't the point! She ain't gon' learn if someone else's picking up after her."

"You don't have to talk about me like I'm not even here." Esperanza said, but Abigail and Bill were too caught in the heat of their argument to pay her any mind.

"It's done." Bill said. "Probably best to make camp here so we don't have to drag this thing." Abigail bit her tongue while Bill started to skin the deer for what it was worth. Esperanza, watching the scene unfold, could barely stand the sight of it.

"Good lord." She squealed.

"Do us a favor and make a campfire, would ya, girl?" Bill asked Esperanza. Any opportunity that kept her attention from the gore unfolding before her was a welcome one, so she did just as he asked. She'd finished drawing the fire just as he wrapped up slicing a few slabs out of the deer. They roasted the meat over the open flames.

Bill handed a piece of cooked meat to her, who wasted no time ripping it out of his grasp and proceeded to chow down. Bill held out a piece to Abigail, who hesitated to take it. He shook the slab in her direction and she begrudgingly took it from his hands. She took a small bite, but as her stomach began to demand more, she couldn't help but keep up with the rest of them.

"How did you even find us?" Esperanza asked.

"You two don't do a very good job of hiding your tracks." He said.

"We weren't trying to." Abigail said.

"I'd be surprised if you were!" Bill bit off enough to feed the three of them.

"What could we have done better?" Esperanza asked him.

Abigail shot her a look, they didn't need him at all, let alone his advice but she held her tongue and continued to eat.

"You could try circling back into your own tracks.

That's liable to throw most anyone for a loop." He said. Jules's whimper caught Bill's attention. "This ain't for you, ya mutt." He told her, but Jules's gaze remained unbroken, filled with hope that the big scruffy human might bless her with a share of the spoils. Bill groaned as he got up and walked back to the deer. He reached into its sliced open chest and ripped off a rib. "Here." He threw down the rib. It didn't have a chance to hit the ground before Jules caught it. Bill laughed.

When they set out the next morning, it wasn't but a few hours before they arrived at Pike's Basin. They stood atop a massive cliff edge and looked down on what may have been a raging river many centuries ago but was nothing more now than dirt and a few scant trees, save for the tiny shack dwarfed by its rocky surroundings below. They spotted half a dozen horses hitched outside as smoke billowed out the chimney.

"This is it." Bill said.

That was enough for Abigail.

"How do we know that's them down there?" Esperanza asked.

"All things considered? We don't." Bill replied.

"We ought to make sure we know who we're dealing with." Esperanza said.

"I don't disagree with ya, little missy. But with a band of killers, it ain't so simple as knocking on the door and askin' who's home."

"How else would you know?" She asked.

"We've gots to be careful, is all. Ain't no way of knowing if they're the type to shoot first and ask questions later." As he turned his attention back to the shack at the bottom of the basin, he noticed something out of the corner of his eye. Someone was approaching the cabin. He looked back up, only to realize that only Esperanza and Jules were beside him. Abigail, it seems, had gone ahead.

"What the hell is she doing?" He muttered. They watched from afar as Abigail planted her feet in the ground outside the shack.

"Joseph Bacall!" She shouted, her call echoing throughout the chasm.

"Who's askin'?" A voice called out from the shack.

"I don't recall askin' nothing!" She said.

"You after that bounty, aren't ya?" He, who she could only presume was Joe, asked.

"That's right."

"I'll give you one chance to turn around! It ain't ended too well for the other folks that tried." She looked down at the ground, to the three rotting corpses that laid face down in the dirt outside the shack.

"I see." She said. "Tell ya what, I'll give *you* one chance."

"One chance for what?"

"To die on your feet like a man." The whole time they'd been shouting at each other, one of the Bacall boys was lining up his shot with a long rifle, out the front window of the shack. As he readied to pull the trigger, sunlight hit the silver tip of his rifle. The glint caught Abigail's eye. She was quick to draw her pistol, and she fired.

"This girl's got a death wish!" Bill shouted as he ran down into the gully after her. Esperanza and Jules trailed behind him.

Abigail pressed forward, toward the shack, as bullets blasted out from within it and flew past her. She managed to shoot dead the gunner in the window, as well as the poor soul that emerged out the front door with a rifle in hand who didn't let off so much as a single shot before he fell dead to the ground. She reloaded her pistol as she stomped onto the porch, and once all six shots were loaded, she kicked down the door and blasted away at everyone inside. By the time Bill and Esperanza finally made it all the way down to the shack, she'd made quick work of the entire Bacall gang.

"Good lord, Abigail." Bill said.

"What was that about getting myself killed?" She asked him as she dragged one of the bodies out of the shack and into the dirt.

"When you're right, you're right." Bill said. He assisted her with dragging the rest of the bodies out of the shack.

"You have a taste for violence, don't you?" Esperanza asked her as she watched them load the bodies up onto the backs of the horses.

Abigail looked at her but had nothing to say.

The three of them carried two bodies each on the back of their horses, and Bill drug another horse by the reins behind him as they rode back to Ridgewood. They rode through the day and into the night, eventually making it to the sheriff's station. The sheriff stepped out and watched on as Bill and Abigail dropped the bodies at his feet.

"Well, ain't that something." He said as he looked Joeseph Bacall in his glassy dead eyes, piled atop the rest of his buddies. "I believe I owe you a bounty," he said, looking at Bill.

"Actually, you owe *me* a payment." Abigail clarified.

"You?" The sheriff asked.

"By myself."

The sheriff looked at Bill, who confirmed the claim with a nod.

"Well, I'll be damned." The sheriff retreated into the station to collect the cash. When he returned, he handed the stack to Abigail.

"Much obliged." She said with a tip of her hat. She thumbed through the stack to count it.

"I'd say at least half of that's mine." Bill said.

"You didn't do a goddamn thing!" Abigail shouted.

"I helped you cart 'em over here, didn't I?" He said.

"You're getting two horses! You've got more than enough." She said as she shoved the stacks of cash into her pocket.

Further down the street, Wesley found himself carried out of the saloon. One too many patrons felt he was cheating at cards, and so he was no longer welcome inside. After cursing the owner to high hell, he lit a cigarette and grumbled to himself. He took a drag as Abigail's argument with Bill echoed down the street. He thought nothing of it at first, but his attention was fully captured when he saw them approaching the stable, with Esperanza behind them.

"I guess this is where we part ways." Bill said as he led the last of his new horses into their pens.

"I guess it is." Abigail said.

"Hey, Lil' Hope." Wesley said.

The three of them turned toward the front of the stable to see him standing in the doorway.

"Who the hell are you?" Bill asked.

"Her family." He pointed at Esperanza. "Let's go."

"She ain't going nowhere." Abigail stepped in front of Esperanza to shield her from him.

"Nobody has to get hurt if we settle this right here

and now." Wesley said.

"We'll settle this right here and now, but no one getting hurt is a stretch." Abigail's hand hovered over her gun.

"You sure that's how you wanna play this?" Wesley's finger twitched over his gun.

"It's the only way I know how." They stared at each other in silence. Wesley was the first to draw his gun, but Abigail was quick on the draw and she gunned him down.

"Sorry for the mess." She said, holstering her gun.

"Did you have to do it in here?" He asked.

"Did it look like he was giving me much of an option?"

"Help me get him outta here."

The two of them dragged the body toward Abigail's horse, hitched outside. Esperanza watched as they pulled him across the dirt, his vacant dead eyes bore a hole right through her. Wesley would often be the one to talk Colin down from the fit of rage he sought to take out on the girl. It also wasn't long ago that he'd returned from one of many nights out with Colin, covered in blood that belonged to neither of them. That happened more often than not, and despite what Wesley may have done for her, she had to remind herself of what the lot of them did *to* her.

Esperanza, Abigail and Bill rode on horseback

out of town to a nearby riverbank. They disposed of him in the river, letting the current carry him downstream.

"You best get outta here," he warned them. "Lord knows how close behind his friends are."

"Thanks, Bill."

"Oh, don't get sentimental on me now." He grumbled.

"Really. Thank you. For everything." She hugged him. He embraced her.

"Take care of yourself."

"Likewise."

Abigail mounted her horse and rode off with Esperanza. Jules found it difficult to keep up with them as she hobbled in their wake.

"I told you she'd be a problem!" Abigail said.

Esperanza brought her horse to a stop. She dismounted and picked the dog up off the ground and seated her atop the horse. She got back on and they rode, Jules's tongue flapping out of her mouth with a wide grin on her face as they rode on and the wind blew past them. Abigail rolled her eyes as they continued forth.

7

Ridgewood far behind them, Abigail and Esperanza made camp in the woods shortly after they crossed the Texas border. Horses hitched to a nearby tree, the pair of them took their rest on opposite sides of the campfire. Jules lay curled up at Esperanza's feet. Abigail stared at the night sky, a brilliant blanket that stitched together an unfathomable amount of stars. To her side, Esperanza giggled as she read a dime novel.

"What are you laughing about?" Abigail asked.

"This story I'm reading is very comical," she said. "A roguish explorer uncovers treasures from ancient civilizations, and he's got a wit about him."

"Why do you waste your time reading fanciful trash?" Abigail turned to her.

"It's no Jules Verne, but I'd hardly resort to calling it trash."

"Where'd you even get that?"

"*Borrowed* it from Bill," she confessed, almost hiding behind the pages of the book.

"Borrowed?" Abigail huffed.

"Did you just laugh?" Esperanza asked.

"No."

"Are you sure?"

"Ain't no good gon' come from fillin' your head with the ideas of others," Abigail said.

"Where's all this vitriol springing from? Did a book convince your husband to leave you?"

"You best watch your tongue, girl."

"You seem so aggressive in your stance against escapism."

"The sooner you realize there is no escape, the better off you'll be." It wasn't but a moment when the motive behind Abigail's contempt finally dawned on Esperanza.

"Now I get it."

"Get what?" Abigail sat upright.

"You can't read, can you?" She asked.

"I don't need to read."

"But if you had to, you couldn't?"

Abigail had no reply.

"No wonder you made me read the handbill," she muttered.

"Go to bed, girl." Abigail turned away from the fire and laid back down. "We're up at dawn."

Esperanza couldn't help but laugh to herself and continued reading on. She was hard to awaken the next morning, tired from spending too much time enjoying a vicarious adventure. After a good shove from Abigail she was awake, and the pair of them readied their horses for another day's journey. As they trotted along down a dirt road, Jules followed on the ground, her leg having mostly healed by now. Something caught her attention though, and she planted her paws in the ground and started to growl.

"What is it, girl?" Esperanza asked. Jules had made eye contact with a rabbit, and they stared each other down. As Esperanza followed the dog's line of sight to the tiny creature, she knew it was already too late. Jules bolted, and despite Esperanza calling out to her, the beast couldn't be stopped. The rabbit hopped away into the thick brush with blazing speed, but Jules kept up with it. The forest too dense for her to follow on horseback, Esperanza dismounted and ran after them.

"Girl!" Abigail shouted, but she too, could not be stopped.

Jules flew over fallen logs, ducked and weaved through the labyrinthine structure of the piney wood—refusing to let up in her pursuit. The rabbit made her work for it, hopping away with incredible grace and blazing speed. Esperanza trailed behind them, failing to keep up with their pace. With the speed Jules displayed, it was hard to believe her leg had been injured just a few short weeks earlier. The distance between predator and prey shrunk with every inch Jules gained, until the rabbit unwittingly hopped into a trap.

A net sprung out from underneath a pile of leaves, scooping up the rabbit from below and suspending it from the branch of a tree. Jules barked to high hell underneath the rabbit as it dangled above her. From behind a tree, an old woman held the rope that carried the critter in the air.

"Go on, dog!" She shouted. "Git!"

"Hey!" Esperanza finally caught up to them.

"This your dog?" The old woman barked.

"That's right." Esperanza replied. "Jules!" The dog was quick to hush.

"Well, I suppose I should be thanking her." The old woman approached Jules and patted her on the head. Jules panted with a grin upon receipt of the old woman's affection. "She helped me catch supper."

"You just wait here until something crawls through your trap?" She asked.

"Heavens, no! I'd likely starve to death if I did that! I was just about through setting up this trap when I saw providence hopping my way. Come to think of it, you best exercise caution on your way back. You may end up in another one of these!" She pointed at the net that swung above their heads. She lowered the trap and took the rabbit in hand.

She unsheathed a knife from her belt.

Abigail had finally caught up to them, arriving upon the sight of a strange old woman brandishing a knife in front of Esperanza. She was quick to raise her rifle.

"Don't even think about it!" She shouted.

"Good lord, woman!" The old lady said. "Is that how you greet everybody?" Abigail spotted the rabbit in the woman's other hand.

"What's going on here?" Abigail lowered her weapon.

"I was just thanking your daughter for helping me catch this little guy." The old woman took the knife and slit the rabbit's throat.

Esperanza shuddered.

"She's not my daughter." Abigail clarified.

"Oh." The old woman said.

"We really ought to get going." Abigail told Esperanza.

"Nonsense, girls! You helped me catch supper. Why not join me for some?"

"Can we?" Esperanza asked Abigail.

"We wouldn't want to intrude." Abigail said, doing her best to navigate the semantic landscape and avoid upsetting the strange old woman currently wielding a bloody knife.

"Oh heaven's no. My husband loves company. Come!" She walked away. Esperanza looked to

Abigail for approval, and Abigail rolled her eyes.

"Gotta get the horses first."

Esperanza smiled. After they returned from grabbing the horses, they led their steeds by the reins as the old woman shepherded them all toward her home.

"What's your name, Miss?" Esperanza asked.

"Evelyn." It wasn't long at all before they'd arrived at the cabin. "You can hitch 'em up here." She pointed to a post by the front porch. After they hitched the horses, Esperanza stepped onto the porch to follow Evelyn inside but Abigail lagged a bit as she looked around at their surroundings. She noticed what looked like the skulls and bones of small animals, dangling from the branches of the trees that surrounded them.

"Where's your husband, Evelyn?" Abigail asked.

"Just inside! Come!"

Abigail approached the door behind them. She stopped Esperanza from entering, as a putrid stench stung Abigail's nose. Abigail entered first, just in case. Inside the cozy quarters, they saw a single bed up against the wall, a shelf with maybe two dozen books and the various trophies of wild game adorning the wall. The smell they'd encountered outside was even more potent in here and Abigail physically recoiled from the repugnance.

"Robert! We have company!" Evelyn called out. Abigail and Esperanza looked around for her husband. The décor was unassuming enough, with the exception of the rotting corpse sitting on a chair in the corner of the cabin, whom they could only presume was once Robert. Both Abigail and Esperanza looked at each other, wondering what exactly they'd managed to get themselves into this time. Evelyn walked over to Robert and leaned in.

"Don't be rude, Robbie. Say hi!" She told him.

Dead silence.

"Isn't he a trip?" Evelyn asked them with a grin.

"There's a word for it." Abigail said.

"Come, sit!" Evelyn extended a hand toward the table in the middle of the cabin.

The girls took heavy steps toward the table, each of them pondering whether it was indeed too late to turn down supper but before they could arrive at an answer, they'd already dragged out their chairs and took their seats. Evelyn stoked the fire in the fireplace, and once it was good and hot, she crossed over to the table to prepare the rabbit.

"How long have you two been together?" Esperanza asked her.

"Ever since we were kids!" Evelyn said. "Both our families owned plots of land just beside each other. They weren't too keen on Robbie and I getting together, and they did their damndest to try and keep us away from each other. But love ain't so quick to die, ain't it Robbie?"

Again, silence.

"We ended up runnin' away together," she continued. "Haven't spent a day apart since! We built this cabin ourselves, you know."

"He doesn't say much, does he?" Abigail asked her.

"He always has been somewhat taciturn." She slid all the ingredients into a pot and carried it over to the fire. Esperanza shifted in her chair and recoiled from the shock of something unnaturally frigid beneath the wooden table. She leaned over to get a look at what she'd brushed against and shot straight back up in her chair at the sight of it. Abigail's brow furled, and Esperanza pointed down at the table.

Abigail leaned over much the same to take a look, and noticed a double barrel shotgun strapped to the bottom of the table. *This just keeps getting better,* Abigail thought. Evelyn, now finished with the stew, approached the table with two bowls in hand. She placed them out in front of the girls.

"Dig in!" she said.

"Thanks!" Esperanza looked down at the bowl of dull brown *something* that lay before her. Abigail pushed the soup around with her wooden spoon. Esperanza, always the adventurous one, carefully brought the spoon to her lips and let the liquid drip onto her tongue, seemingly one drop at a time. She went from drops to sips, and quickly transitioned to scarfing it down by the spoonful. This was a surprising turn of events that unfolded in front of Abigail, though not nearly as surprising as walking into a strange woman's cabin to find her husband rotting in a corner chair. Abigail tasted a spoonful of soup herself, and quickly understood what had Esperanza so ravenous. Evelyn may have been off her rocker, but she damn well knew how to stew.

Evelyn took her seat at the head of the table with a bowl of her own. Before she could take her first sip, she slammed her spoon down on the table like a gavel. Abigail and Esperanza jumped at the sound of it.

"Robert! There's no need to be so rude!" She shouted.

"You two don't get much company around here?" Abigail asked her.

"Not often, no." She said. "Frankly, it's been some time since I cooked for more than just the two of us."

"Do you ever think about life without Robbie?" Abigail asked her.

"Why would I have to?" Evelyn replied.

Jules began to growl.

"What is it, Jules?" Esperanza asked. Abigail looked over her shoulder to the window behind her. There were men approaching the cabin from the forest.

"Jules?" Evelyn asked Esperanza.

"Yes ma'am." She said with a smile.

"As in Verne?" Evelyn asked. Esperanza lit up.

"That's right!"

"Shit." Abigail muttered. The McCalister gang had followed them here.

"What's the matter?" Evelyn asked.

"We've been followed." She said.

"Friends of yours?" Evelyn asked.

"Hardly." Abigail replied.

"What do we do?" Esperanza asked.

Evelyn stood up from her chair and crossed the cabin over to a hatch by Robert's feet. She swung it open.

"Hide down here." She suggested.

"What about you?" Esperanza asked.

"Don't worry about me," she assured them. "I can handle it."

Esperanza approached the hatch, Jules by her side.

"Leave the dog up here." She instructed. Jules whimpered as Esperanza tried to calm her down.

"It's okay, girl. Stay." The dog sat beside Evelyn as Esperanza and Abigail walked down the steps into the basement underneath the cabin. Evelyn shut the hatch behind them. She took a pelt suspended over the mantle and laid it over the hatch door. After a deep breath, she exited the cabin. Colin and his crew approached.

"Afternoon, gentlemen." She said.

"Good afternoon, ma'am." Colin said.

"What can I do for you?" She asked them.

"We're looking for somebody. Have reason to believe they were headed in this direction." He informed her.

"Looking for who?" If she played dumb enough, she figured, they might not even bother going inside.

Back underneath the cabin, Abigail and Esperanza stood in the cramped space. Light from the cabin crept in from the cracks in the floorboards above them, and a small crack in the baseboard lining the top of the basement let in light from outside.

"How the hell did they find us?" Abigail asked.

"They're good at tracking." Esperanza said.

"Or maybe we're good at leaving an obvious trail." She said.

"There was one time someone in our gang spoke out against Colin. He snuck away from camp while everyone was asleep, but by the next night, Colin had come back with his body in the back of a wagon." Esperanza recalled.

"What could he have possibly said to demand

such a reaction?" Abigail asked.

"Had nothing to do with what he said. It was about sending a message to the rest of us."

Upstairs, Evelyn and Colin entered, a couple of the other gang members following behind them.

"As you can see, gentlemen," she assured them, "It's just my husband and I." She said. Jules barked. "And Jules, of course." She crossed over to pat the dog on the head.

"Woo-hoo, god damn, miss!" Colin shouted. "That's your husband?" He pointed to the corpse.

"That's right."

"It smells to high hell in here." He exclaimed.

"Probably what you dragged in with you." Evelyn said.

"No, I reckon it's dead fucking body in the corner there." He said.

"Don't you talk about Robbie like that!" She yelled. Jules barked at Colin.

"Look, bitch! I know you're lying. You got two horses hitched out there, and I know the other one ain't his! Where is she?" He demanded. Jules refused to pipe down. "Shut that fuckin' dog up." One of his cronies drew a pistol.

Esperanza squeaked at the sight of Jules in trouble and Abigail was quick to cover her mouth, but by that point—it was too late. Colin looked at the floorboards. He got down on his knees and pressed his face to the cracks. They could see his eye as it peered down at them.

Evelyn kicked the table over, grabbing the shotgun underneath it and blasting away one of his gang members. Colin quickly dove out the front window as the rest of his gang returned fire, but Evelyn kept shooting!

Abigail punched the baseboard out and opened it up, wide enough for them to crawl out of. She helped Esperanza up and she wiggled her way out from underneath the house.

"Run, girl!" Abigail shouted. As Evelyn took cover from heavy fire on the front side of the house, Esperanza slipped out the back and ran.

"Come on, Jules!" She shouted, and Jules dove out the same window Colin jumped through. She ran through the firefight and circled around the house. Colin couldn't help but notice the dog rounding the house.

"Cover me." He said to one of his gang members as he ran to follow the dog. Abigail managed to squeeze out from underneath the cabin, and she ran after Jules and Esperanza. Colin rounded the house, saw them attempting to escape and gave chase, shooting his pistol all the way. "Get back here, Esperanza!"

Abigail caught up to her, and the three of them ran as fast as their legs would carry them.

"Don't stop!" Abigail shouted. It wasn't but a second after she said it that they failed to notice the steep drop off they were running straight for, and Esperanza tumbled down into a raging river below. "Swim to the shore!" Abigail shouted, but Esperanza treaded water. Jules didn't hesitate to jump off into the river and swim after her.

"I can't—I can't—" Esperanza tried to say as her head bobbed above and below the water. It was then that Abigail realized the girl couldn't swim. She slid down the hill and dove into the river below. She swam with the current and caught up to Esperanza, taking her in hand to keep her head above water. "Hang onto me!" Abigail told her. She tried to carry her to the shore, but the current carried them straight into a rock. Abigail lost her grip on the girl with the impact and floated further down the river. Esperanza managed to hang onto the rock for dear life.

"Abigail!" Esperanza called out.

"Get out of the water!" She yelled. Esperanza yelled something else at Abigail, but the distance growing between them combined with the roar of the raging rapids made it difficult to hear. "What?" Abigail yelled.

"Waterfall!" Esperanza shouted. Abigail managed to turn herself around and noticed she was being carried to the drop. She tried to swim against the current toward the edges but it was no use. She fell some fifty or sixty feet into a lake below, landing on a rock that sent shockwaves through her bones. Despite her body crying out in pain, she managed to paddle her way over to the shore and just barely dragged herself out of the lake.

She turned over to lie on her back and groaned in agony. She stared at the sky. With every breath she heaved, she could feel her ribs cracking as her chest expanded and retracted. To her side, she could hear someone ride up beside her. She tried to turn her neck, but the pain was so intense that she could do nothing more than lay there motionless. Perhaps Colin would take care of Abigail's problem and bring their short-lived journey to a close. If it would put her out of this pain, both the shock she was currently in and the rest she'd carried for years, it would be most welcome indeed.

The man stood above her, silhouetted against the sun. She could barely make him out. It couldn't have been Colin. As her vision adjusted, she recognized a face that she thought she'd never see again.

"Abby?" Her brother said.

"Benji?" She could hardly believe it. A rugged and aged Benjamin stood above her. Had she already died and dragged herself into the afterlife? They both had a tough time believing the providence that had transpired to reunite them, but before she could squeeze out another word; her head grew weary, her vision began to fade, and she fell unconscious.

8

Abigail awoke in bed with a sharp gasp, air like knives swirling in a storm within her lungs. She held her hand to her chest, every breath she heaved sent waves of pain throughout her body. The only thing that was seemingly keeping her crackling rib cage together was the set of sweaty bandages that ran across her chest. *That's new*, it occurred to her. She looked around to see the tiny bedroom she'd been recovering in. Aside from the cramped bed she was currently laying on, there was a small bedside table next to her. Rain beat down on the only window in the bedroom, but whose bed was this?

"Didn't mean to wake you," she heard a woman say to her. Soothed little by the presence of a stranger, Abigail quickly pushed herself up against the wall to face her. In the doorway she met the gaze of a pregnant woman with a welcoming expression.

"Who are you?" Abigail asked.

"My name is Suzanne," she answered. "I'm your brother's wife."

So that was real, Abigail thought. She attempted to sit up straight on the bed, but winced from her body's cries that she not move at all.

"You beat yourself up pretty good," Suzanne said. "Going over a waterfall, I heard?"

"What can I say?" Abigail said as she shifted into a more tolerable position. "I live for excitement."

"You're lucky Ben found you when he did."

"Where is he?"

"Upstairs. I can go get him if you like."

"I can get him," Abigail declared as she staggered out of bed.

"Easy now," she warned as she crossed the room to assist. "You've been in that bed for nearly three days." Abigail swatted her away.

"Leave me be!" Abigail's arm quaked as she held herself up against the wall.

"Don't be afraid to ask for help, now." Suzanne kept her distance.

Abigail slowly shambled out of the bedroom by hugging the walls, and entered the living room at the base of the stairs. This house was easily twice the size of the one she'd been forced to abandon—almost regal by comparison. Benjamin had done well for himself in the years since they'd seen each other last.

"Where's the girl?" Abigail asked.

"Esperanza?" The girl had a name after all. Abigail nodded.

"She's fine, don't you worry."

"She hasn't been torturing y'all while I've been indisposed, has she?"

"Heavens, no!" Suzanne smiled. "She's a good kid, that one. Hasn't stopped trying to help out around the ranch."

"I suppose it's just me she pesters for sport," Abigail grumbled. Suzanne gave her an awkward laugh.

"Abby." Even if its texture was gruff, roughened by the intervening years, there was no mistaking his voice. She turned to greet him and there at the bottom of the stairs, stood her brother. She dragged herself over to him, and nearly fell in the process. He caught her, his worn hands holding her by the arms. He towered over her, as Benji always did. She laid her head against his chest, and wrapped her arms around him. He hugged her all the same, and Abigail winced from the pain, to which her brother apologized.

"I don't care," she assured him, and she tightened her embrace. This was the first time in over a decade Abigail wasn't plagued with thought—the world was quiet, her mind was clear and Benjamin was *here* and if time allowed, she would stay right here for another ten years.

"Let's get you off your feet," he told her as he helped her walk over to the living room to take a seat in a cushy chair. "I can't believe you're really here." He sat down across from her, Suzanne beside him.

"I'd say the same."

"I thought you were dead," Benjamin said. "I searched the forest around the house for weeks afterward."

"How did you get away from those Injuns?"

"Barely. I had to light the place up to get away, but not before one of them stuck me good." He unbuttoned his shirt to show her the massive scar across his chest. "When I came back with the cavalry," he said as he buttoned his shirt, "they'd taken what they wanted and left. What about you? What happened?"

"That's a very broad question with a very long answer."

"I've got nothing but time for you, Abby."

Of all the days Abigail might needlessly replay, the day the house was attacked was one she hadn't thought about in a long while. She looked to the window as rain beat down upon it.

"I met a boy in the woods."

9

T he rain poured down heavy upon them. Abigail lay on her knees in the mud. She looked up at Sid who loomed above her, clad in black save for the red bandana, with his hand extended toward her. His chiseled features gave the impression that he might've been far older than he actually was, but the truth is he couldn't have been a day older than 17. Her grip on the pistol could only ease the longer she stared up at him. She would've been right to question the happenstance of her meeting with a strange man in the middle of the woods, but Sid had an unmistakably welcoming quality about him. With nowhere to go, everything she'd ever known now up in smoke, she took his hand.

"Let's get you somewhere dry, darling." He told her. She took to her feet. They walked together out of the woods toward a horse drawn covered cart awaiting them on the dirt road. "How'd you end up out here all by your lonesome?" He helped her onto the back of the cart.

"I should ask you the same thing," she replied.

"I ain't alone! I've got Tony!" He ran his hand down the horse's mane. "Say hi, Tony." The horse spit, and Abigail giggled. Sid helped her onto and under the cover of the cart. He took his seat at the front, took the reins in hand and whipped Tony to carry them off. She looked around the empty wooden cart.

"You like to travel light?" she asked.

"Just needed to pop into town real quick. Mundane, really. What about you? What's your story?" He asked.

"My family's farm was raided by injuns. Barely made it out of there alive."

"You the only one that make it out?"

Abigail nodded.

"Damn savages."

"And you?" She asked.

"No disrespect, little lady, but I'd pulled the cart over to relieve myself."

"I suppose God does have a sense of humor about him."

"I ain't so sure about that."

"You think God is humorless?"

"I'd say my need to stop had more to do with the whiskey I had back in town more than anything else."

"Are you a nonbeliever?"

"There's plenty I believe in. Loyalty, family, respect."

"But not God?"

"It's hard to believe there's someone out there that would sit idly by while a young girl was ripped away from her family. And if there is, that don't sound like someone worthy of worship to me."

Abigail didn't know what to say. Her family instilled faith in her from birth and despite a desire to stay curled up in the warmth of her bed when awoken in the early hours of a given Sunday morning; she rode into town every week with her family for church service. For all the hardship her family endured over the years, whether it was countless seasons where the harvest hardly turned a crop or at age 7 when her home burned down with her grandfather trapped inside it; she'd never been compelled to question, let alone consider, why God refused to intervene.

The rain had finally let up as Sid turned off the main road and followed a trail deep into the woods. Before long, they arrived at a small clearing atop a cliff overlooking miles of countryside. Four tents surrounded a fire pit in the middle of camp, with seven or so of Sid's men scattered about. Abigail was the only woman for miles. As they arrived, she got an impression of the gang from first looks:

young or old, all of them were dirty, mean and rugged. Not the kind of men a girl her age would typically surround herself with. Not willfully, anyway.

"Boys, we have a guest!" Sid brought the cart to a stop and stood up on the bench. "This here's Abigail. She's going to be staying with us for a little while."

Abigail raised a hand, but kept it close to her chest, with a wave *hello*.

"Da hell is this, Sid?" One of them asked.

"She's one of us now." Sid explained.

"We hardly got enough to feed ourselves," another toothless crony cried. "Let alone now with you dragging your cooze back to camp!"

"Hey!" He shouted. "Were we not all without a place we could call home at one time or another?"

The gang stood silent. Sid stepped off the cart and began to walk amongst his gang.

"We stick together because the only thing we can count on in this world, is each other. The same here applies to Abigail." He turned to face her. "She's one of us now."

She spent the remainder of the night getting acquainted with everyone at the camp. As the night progressed, it became clear to Abigail that the colorful band of rogues she found herself now a part of was betrayed by the exterior she'd been greeted with when she rolled into camp earlier. Each of them shared incredible stories of lost loves, daring escapes and narrow brushes with death that captivated her until the early morning light. What she came to admire about the men was that despite all of them treading their own paths of hardship, they all managed to find one other, and were stronger because of it.

One among them kept to himself. The whole night while Abigail played audience to the gang's raucous recounting of their various adventures, he sat by himself over by the cliff edge. She'd glance over at him occasionally to see him silhouetted by the pale moon light, his profile illuminated occasionally by the dim orange glow of his cigarillo. As everyone headed off to their tents for some shuteye, she figured to at least introduce herself before heading off to bed.

"Hello there." She might as well have not even been there. "My name's Abigail. What's yours?" He blew a puff of smoke. Sid approached her and put his hands on her shoulders.

"Let's get you to bed," he said. They turned away from the smoker.

"Did I say something to offend him?"

"Who, Bill? Nah, he's just kind of a grouch. Slow to grow on ya, but he's good people." Abigail looked over her shoulder back at him. Was this all he did?

Isolate himself and smoke cigarillos? For what did they keep him around for?

"Normally, this would be my tent, but seeing as we've got a lady staying with us now, I figure it ought to be yours," Sid told her.

"That's awfully kind of you."

"Wouldn't want you to feel discomfort. This here's your new home, for as long as you'd like it to be."

"Thank you, Sid." She gave him a kiss on the cheek. "Good night."

"Good night." Sid smiled.

Abigail retired into the tent. Inside she found a chest, some bottles of alcohol and a thin pad that passed for a bed. She laid down and tried to fall asleep, but the sounds of windows shattering, bullets flying and her brother shouting echoed through her head. How could she have left him? He was the only family she had left, and she chose to run. Now gone, she was the last of the Lamberts, or so she thought. And perhaps Sid and his gang would do for family. For now.

The next morning, Abigail changed out of the tattered, bloodstained dress she'd left home in and traded it for a set of Sid's clothes she found in the chest. Luckily for her, Sid was the scrawny type—his clothes didn't hang off her frame too severely. She tucked a black button up into black trousers, a new look more befitting of the company she now kept. She emerged from the tent to a laugh from Sid.

"Just help yourself, why don't ya?" He said.

"I wanted out of those rags."

"I don't blame ya." He held her hand. "Come with me." They walked together to the far end of the camp.

"What are we doing?"

"I wanna teach you how to shoot."

"I know how to shoot a gun!" Had he forgotten how they met?

"Good! Then I won't have much to teach you." They arrived at for what passed for a shooting range: a few empty bottles of whiskey resting atop a fallen log about ten yards from where she stood. Sid took his gun and handed it to her.

"I've got a gun." She pulled out her revolver. Sid holstered his weapon. She took aim.

"Don't be afraid of it."

"I ain't!"

"You have to think of the gun as a part of you." She looked at him, befuddled.

"What kinda nonsense is that?"

"The kind that'll help your aim."

It was certainly one of the more ridiculous things she'd ever heard before, but she took the suggestion in earnest. As she lined up her shot, she focused less on the gun in her hand and more on the power in her arm. She took a deep breath through her nostrils and fired. The bottle shattered! She laughed.

"See what I told you!" He said.

She twirled around, even for a beginner, it was quite the shot. Abigail locked eyes with him and the distance between them closed, they were mere inches apart now. She could still feel the rush of the blast as it coursed through her body. She might very well allow him to kiss her—if only Bill hadn't stepped in and interrupted their moment.

"Sid!" He shouted. "We're burning daylight."

"Be there in a minute!"

Bill retreated back to the covered wagon at the mouth of the camp.

"He talks." Abigail said.

"You should hear him liquored up. Liable to break out into song."

"Are you going somewhere?"

"We've got some work to do today." He walked over to the wagon. Abigail followed.

"What kinda work?" She asked.

"It's a good opportunity for the family. It'll keep us going for a good long while."

"Why are you being so cagey?"

He turned to face her. "Cagey?"

"You're not giving me any straight answers."

Sid mulled it over for a moment. "Come with us." He said.

"Sid," Bill butted in, "no."

"Was I talking to you?"

Bill spit.

"I'd love to," she said. Sid laughed and gently touched her chin with his fist.

"You're great, you know that?" Now Abigail smiled. "But listen here—it's vital you do whatever I say when we get there. There won't be no time for questioning." Abigail nodded. He smiled. Bill brushed the hair of the horse pulling the cart. Sid took his seat at the front of the wagon.

"You sure this is how you wanna play this?" Bill asked him.

"We gotta see what she can do, right?"

"Not if it's the last thing we do," he said to the horse.

"Just drive," Sid said. Bill grumbled as he took his seat with the reins in hand. They rode for some time until they arrived in Blackwater; the very same Abigail had ridden into several times with her mother for supplies not too long ago. They pulled up the dirt road toward the bank and parked the wagon just outside it. Abigail hopped off the back and circled around to Sid's side.

"You're gonna wanna put that on." He handed her a red bandana. She wrapped it around her hair and Sid laughed. "Oh, you sweet thing." He stepped down from the cart and undid the bandana, tying it around her neck and lifting it over her nose to conceal her face with it.

"What are we doing, Sid?" She asked him.

"What did I say?" He lifted his own bandana over his nose. "No more questions."

Bill stepped off the cart and lumbered over to them, his face already under the cover of his bandana. They readied their guns, and Sid kicked down the door. It fell onto the last man in the line of patrons snaking from the door to the lone teller behind the counter.

"Alright, ladies and gentlemen," he shouted as they stepped over the door. "Surrender your valuables, nobody get any bright ideas and we can all come out of this with our heads in tact!" Sid looked down at the poor guy lying motionless underneath the door he'd just freed from its hinges. "Well, maybe except him."

Bill waved his gun toward the patrons in line, getting them to throw whatever they were in the bank to deposit down into his bag.

"Let's go!" Sid shouted at the teller. He directed him with his gun. "To the vault!"

"Now sir, I—" the teller protested.

"Don't be a hero, old man!" Abigail shouted. "Just open the door!"

Bill craned his head to look at her with wide eyes. The teller crossed over from behind the desk and opened the door to let them in. He led them over to the vault, reluctantly opened it, and Sid pushed him out of the way. Abigail kept her gun on the teller as Sid pilfered the tiny vault of every last dollar he could carry. He crossed over to Bill and stuffed the money in his sack. Bill's ear perked up.

"I hear the law," he said.

"Much obliged everybody!" Sid yelled as he took a bow before everyone they'd just robbed. They ran out of the bank, hopped into the wagon and sped away, but not before they attracted a pair of lawmen that tailed them on horseback. Bullets flew past their heads as Abigail and Bill returned fire from the back of the cart, Sid whipping the horses to ride as fast as their shoes would carry them. Bill fired and hit one of their horses. It tripped up and the lawman atop went flying. Abigail fired, again and again until she managed to hit the other lawman in the chest. He fell back onto the ground, and she gasped as she watched his body fold when he hit the dirt at high speed.

Abigail remained quiet for the ride back to camp, replaying the sight of the fallen officer over and over again in her head. They pulled into camp and Sid threw down the bag of cash on the ground at his family's feet. They tore into the bag like a pack of hungry dogs with fresh meat, all taking part in the triumphant revelry that came with a new score. Abigail found it difficult not to smile as she watched the joy radiate amongst the entire camp.

"Somebody open a bottle of the good shit!" Sid proclaimed. "Tonight, we celebrate!"

"Do we even have good shit to open?" Bill asked.

"If we don't," Sid said as he grabbed a wad of bills out of the sack, "it ain't like we can't afford it!" He laughed.

One of them cracked open a crate of whiskey and they all had a merry time regaling each other around the campfire. The energy was positively infectious, and as Sid looked around to soak in the rare moment of jubilation, he noticed that everyone in camp was taking part in the celebration, even Bill was enjoying his drink enough to start getting musical. But one among them was missing, sitting by her lonesome inside of her tent. Sid pulled back the tarp to find her sitting on the floor as she quietly cried to herself.

"What's the matter, sweetheart?" He asked her. She was quick to wipe the tears from her face and hushed herself upon the realization that she was no longer alone.

"How do you live with it?" she asked.

"Live with what?"

"The suffering."

"Life is suffering, Abigail. We can choose to be weighed down by that, or we can act in spite of it. Everything I do for this family is in that spirit."

"That man," she whispered.

"What man?"

"The man I shot. I killed a man today, Sid."

"Well, we don't know that. Maybe you just clipped him." He took a knee beside her.

"That man probably had a wife. Children. And I took him away from them."

"Hey now." He reached over and gently turned her head so she would meet his gaze. "That man was trying to take you away from me. But it was either him or you. This life we lead, it's full of tough choices. But I know without a shadow of a doubt, I definitely wouldn't want to find myself in a world without you in it."

"You mean that?" She sniffled.

"As long as we're looking out for each other, nothing will stop us darling." She smiled and leaned toward him. Her lip quivered as the distance between them shrank, and when their lips finally touched, she melted into his arms. She pined for nothing more than to be locked in the comforting safety of this moment for eternity. As she took off her clothes, she knew they would ride together to the ends of the Earth. What she couldn't know then was what awaited her on the road to that end, but for now it wouldn't matter. She was Sid's and Sid was hers, and that was the only thing in this world that mattered.

So much so, no amount of robbing and killing could sway Abigail's determination to her new-found clan. Once an area would get too hot for them to hang around in, the family would ride out to a new spot untainted by their crimes and start the process all over again: rob the nearest town, kill anyone that crossed them, spend every cent of the spoils on hedonistic pleasures, ride out to the next town and repeat. As Abigail sunk deeper into her newly acquired taste for violent thrills, she found herself not only in Sid's arms, but in the arms of anyone in camp that would have her. She lived free, and she treated her body with the same amount of carnal liberty.

At least with those whom he considered family, Sid was not the jealous type, and they all shared in the spoils he brought to them, including now Abigail. The only one who refused her advances was Bill. She'd matured at an incredible pace in the four or so years that Abigail rode with the gang, such was the case for anyone choosing to live outside the law in the manner in which she did. However, he found it would likely be impossible for him to ever see her as anything other than the dirty and scared little girl that Sid had dragged into camp.

What she chose to do with herself was beyond his control, but he wouldn't willfully participate in such degradation. She was doing a fine enough job of that on her own.

While she may have deluded herself enough in the beginning under the guise of living free, the only option to numb herself from the depths of her own corruption would force her to pick up the pace on the hedonic treadmill. Any thought contrary to her chosen path could be swiftly deafened by a deluge of sex, drink or violence. She went to bed drunk most nights just to quiet the voices. The further she sank—the more she drank. Drunk off her own decadence, she could've lived this way forever until she was smacked out of her depraved daze by reality, as it always does. And there she would be presented a choice: sink further or climb out of this hole she'd been digging for the last four years. Most nights, she fell in line with the grooves of habit and chose the former. Until one night, Sid forced her hand.

Though the body count they left in their wake may have said otherwise, Abigail's taste for violence was no match for Sid's, who grew more ruthless and wicked as the years went on. Drastic actions taken for the 'good of the family' in the early days became the norm, and the level at which violence was doled out only continued to rise as they pushed themselves further into the fringes of society. For the longest time, she could only see Sid as the welcoming boy with an open heart that she'd met in the forest all those years ago, and even if he had strayed from the path—she felt that he could be redeemed. Even if she was the only one who could do it, or would even consider the attempt and it was one such evening Abigail was compelled by circumstance to try.

Sid, Abigail and a couple other members of the family rode down a dirt road in the middle of the night when they spotted something curious up ahead.

"What is that?" One of them said. Sid pulled out a pair of binoculars and took a look. The sight of it alone made him laugh with its potential.

"What?" Abigail asked him, but he had no reply. His imagination ran wild with the possibility of what could be awaiting them. Sid ignored her completely, trailed close behind by the rest of the posse.

"What have we got here?" Sid asked as he rode up to the stagecoach.

"We don't want any trouble," the driver said. Sid whistled and twirled his fist around in the air. His two goons picked up speed and passed the coach, blocking the road up ahead with their horses. Everyone came to a halt. Abigail watched from atop her horse as Sid dismounted his own, and approached the man.

"There won't be any trouble if you keep those ears open and don't get any bright ideas." She'd heard him say it a thousand times at this point, and it was almost a thousand times over that trouble seemed to find them.

"We don't have much," he pleaded. "Honest."

"I'll be the judge of that. Search 'em." The goons blocking the road dismounted their horses and approached the back of the stage. They hopped on board and kicked the man's wife and two children out of the coach as they rifled around for any valuables. Abigail could hardly bear the sight of it, they had plenty of food back at the camp, and she could tell Sid was motivated purely by the sport of it all. She rode up beside him.

"What are we doing here, Sid?" She asked him.

"Just seeing what we can find." He spotted the wife and children trying to keep their distance from the cart and he aimed his gun at them. "All of y'all! Against the coach!" The husband stepped down from the bench at the front and joined his family in the lineup. "What have we got, boys?"

"Some cans of beans. Couple blankets." One of them replied.

"Anything worth a damn?" Sid asked.

"Nothin'!"

"I told you sir, we ain't got much." He met Sid's intense gaze.

"Now that there's a problem." He smacked the man across the face with the butt of his revolver.

"Stop it!" Abigail shouted.

"Don't be instructing me, girl!" He shouted back. With Sid's attention turned to Abigail, the husband quickly picked up a nearby rock. His wife shook her head, praying he'd have the good sense to drop the rock and just let the gang do whatever they planned to do—with the hope compliance would be their best chance to escape. Alas, answered her prayers were not and he charged at Sid to smack him upside the head with the stone. Sid turned on a dime and shot the man dead just before he could make contact. His wife cried out, fell to her knees and crawled in the dirt toward her husband who was bleeding out on the floor. The children stood frozen as they witnessed the scene unfold.

"You monster!" The woman shouted at Sid, who towered above her.

"Oh, shut up." He shot the woman in the head. Abigail could hardly believe it herself.

"What the fuck are you doing?" She dismounted her horse. The kids were beginning to cry and Sid lumbered toward them. Abigail tried to hold him back.

"Spare them, please!" She begged.

"What for? This is mercy." Sid brought up his revolver and shot the boy in the head, painting the stagecoach behind him with his blood. Abigail planted her feet in the ground between Sid and the girl.

"Let her go!"

"Get out of my way." Sid said. Abigail aimed her gun at him. "Think very carefully about what you're doing," he warned her.

"The girl leaves." Her grip on the gun was unwavering.

"Fine." Sid lowered his weapon. The girl looked at Sid, then up at Abigail. She lowered her gun and turned to her. Abigail nodded.

"Go." She assured her. She nodded and began to run away from the devastation down the dirt road. It wasn't but a moment before Sid brought his gun back up and shot the girl in the back.

"You bastard!" Abigail shouted as she beat on Sid's back with her fists. He turned and smacked her across the face, cracking her nose. She fell to the ground as the blood poured out of her nostrils in torrents. Sid leaned down and looked her square in the eye.

"If you cross me in front of someone that ain't the family *ever* again, you're gonna end up like her. Understand?"

"You're an animal." She said.

"We're all animals, Abigail. We just like to tell ourselves we're different from the others."

That night she burst into the tent she shared with Sid as soon as they returned to the camp. She crossed right over to her chest and took it in hand.

"Just what do you think you're doing?" He asked her.

"I'm leaving."

"Yeah?" He scoffed. "Where?"

"Anywhere but here." She tried to stomp out of there but Sid blocked her exit. "Move," she demanded.

"*Where* are you going?" He asked again.

"That ain't none of your damn business."

"You don't go anywhere unless I let you, you hear?"

"You ain't my Daddy!"

"No, I ain't. But it is my family. And what I say—goes."

"This ain't no family, it's a pack of animals. If a gang of killers that gun down innocent people is what you call family, that ain't no family I wanna be a part of."

He continued to block the exit, and Abigail dropped her chest on his toes. He groaned and his expression shifted from indignant to furious. Before she could pick up the chest and slip away, he grabbed her by the shirt, punched her in the face and she fell to the ground.

"Don't moralize and pretend you ain't gotta taste for violence, girl." He undid his belt and slid off his pants. Abigail started to crawl backward, away from him, but he lurched over her and held her down by the wrists. "Family sticks together." He had his way with her. She cried for him to stop, but he covered her mouth with his hand. "Quiet," he whispered as she continued to squeak out muffled cries through his fingers. As she lay there, victim to whatever pleasure Sid would extract from her body, she floated above the assault—as if looking down upon the scene which she'd found herself in. How could this happen? Why was this happening? And, most important of all, how could she make sure it would never happen again?

When he was through having his way with her, she turned to her side and sobbed quietly, her face covered in cuts and bruises from Sid's grip down her arms and chest. He stood above her as he got dressed, not a word spoken between them, when one of his goons entered the tent.

"Sid, what—" He spotted Abigail on the floor. "Oh."

"Whaddaya want?" Sid asked.

"We gotta talk about the grave in Reedy Creek."

"Right this moment?"

"I could give you about *ten thousand* reasons why

we ought to."

Sid looked over his shoulder, down at Abigail.

"Get out of here, girl," he commanded. She dressed herself in the tattered rags that were left of her clothes and did as she was told. She exited the tent, and crossed the camp over to Bill's tent. She found him sitting legs crossed, hunched over as he cleaned out his six shooter. A disheveled Abigail poked her head into the tent, and Bill looked up at her.

"You get in a fight with a rose bush?" As she stepped further into the tent, he could see how bruised she really was, and his smile faded.

"Good lord, girl. What happened to you?"

"Sid." She said.

"You let him do that to you?"

"What choice do I have?"

"You're still young girl. You've got a whole life ahead of you."

"What do you expect me to do?"

"It ain't got nothin' with what *I* expect from you. This life's about you, in just the same way this life's about me. The longer you wait for someone to tell you what to do with your life, the more bruises you'll incur."

"I'm gonna get bruised no matter what I do." She rubbed her arms.

"Fair enough. But you've gotta ask yourself if

you're gonna be the one to pick your bruises. Cause you're gonna get 'em either way, and if you don't pick 'em, somebody else will."

"Thank you, Bill," she said. He nodded. She drifted out of his tent and mulled over what he had to say. She sat by the firepit at the heart of the camp and stared into the flames. She bore deep into its flickering rage, and saw the dark shades of what life further down this road had to offer her. As she imagined how much more terror she could possibly sink further into, she overheard Sid's conversation back in the tent.

"The longer we leave it sitting there, the more we're just asking for someone to come and scoop it up." She heard his goon say.

"Who's grave is it?" Sid asked.

"Manco."

"Macno what?"

"That's it."

"Just Manco?"

"I didn't name the fucker. I just know what he's buried with."

"We'll ride out with a couple of the boys at dawn," Sid said.

"I don't think we can afford to wait that long," she heard, but by this point, Abigail had heard enough.

Later that night, long after Abigail and Sid crawled into bed together and the camp drifted off to sleep, she stayed awake. As Sid slumbered beside her, she slipped out of bed and crept out of the tent, successfully leaving Sid's sleep undisturbed. She entered into Bill's tent to wake him up, but just as her hand hovered above him to shake him awake, he was quick on the draw and she stumbled backward onto the floor.

"Good lord!" Bill said. "You know better than to come creepin' inna man's tent in the dead of night, don't ya?"

"I want out, Bill." She dusted herself off.

"Out where?"

"Out of here."

"God be with you." He turned back over to sleep. She stood up.

"I know you want out, too."

"You don't know nothin' about me, girl."

"How old do you want to be, still living like this?"

"I've made my choices." He turned to face her. "You still have time to make yours."

"If you had my kinda time, what would you do with it?"

"Starting fresh?" He pondered the thought. "I'd buy a stable."

"And you can't do that now?"

"Well, not *right* now."

"If not now, when?"

"I don't need you filling my head with fanciful

ideas."

"It's only fanciful if you let it stay an idea."

"Maybe when it starts raining cash."

"What if I told you I could get you enough money to start over?"

"I'd ask you to pass me whatever you've been drinking."

"I'm serious."

"How much we talking?"

"Something like ten thousand dollars."

"And your take?"

"I just want a ride into Caliga Hill."

"Let me get this straight, you're offering me ten grand—for a *ride*?"

"Yeah?"

"Clearly, I'm still dreaming."

"Do you want to help me or not?"

"I still don't see how I fit into all this."

"I'm not getting out of here without Sid getting tipped off. He might sooner kill me than let me go."

"And what do you think he's gonna do to me when he finds out I'm the one that helped you?"

"That's why you get to keep all the money."

"You know, I find that when something sounds too good to be true, it often is."

"Usually. But there ain't nothing usual about me, now is there?"

"I'll give you that."

It wasn't much later that Bill collected what little things he had to take with him and loaded up the stagecoach to ride out. Abigail hid in the cart underneath a couple of blankets, and they rode out without so much as waking anyone. Once Bill reached the perimeter of the camp; he encountered the one gang member still awake, keeping watch as the others slept.

"Going somewhere?" he asked.

"Supply run," Bill replied.

"At this hour?"

"I wanna get there before sunrise."

"Sid's cool with you going alone?" The goon asked as he approached the stagecoach, walking around to the back.

"Are we gonna have a problem, boy?" The goon looked up and met Bill's gaze. If Bill pushed this any further, he'd have to wake up Sid, and that might make for even more trouble than if he just let Bill go.

"Get outta here!"

Bill rode off. Abigail stayed under cover for a good long while, just to make sure that she wouldn't be spotted for whatever reason. As she felt the cart come to a stop, she emerged from underneath the blankets and looked around. Bill had parked the cart at the entrance of a small cemetery. She spotted the creek lining one edge of the cemetery, opposite a tall hill with a church overlooking.

"This ain't Caliga Hill!" She said as she climbed down from the back of the stagecoach.

"That it ain't." Bill said as he hopped off the cart and grabbed his lantern.

"Why did you bring me here?" She asked him.

"Cause how am I supposed to know you were telling the truth?"

"Have I ever given you reason not to trust me?"

"We're a roving band of thieves and killers."

"And?" Bill accepted that the kid was just too dense and grabbed a shovel out of the back of the cart. He threw it at her. She managed to catch it.

"What's this for?"

"I'll give you one guess." Abigail grumbled to herself as she walked along the graves, searching for their best chance at escaping this lifestyle they found themselves trapped in. Bill turned his light toward the headstones as they searched. Abigail continued walking as Bill stopped to read one of the headstones.

"We're looking for Manco, right?" he asked her.

"That's right."

"You just walked past it."

"It's dark." She walked back over to him. "Couldn't see it."

"Sure."

Abigail began to dig.

"Feel free to help," she said.

"You look like you've got it under control." He stood at the foot of the grave and smoked a cigarillo as he watched her dig. Drenched in sweat and dirt all over her body, it was some time before her shovel finally struck the coffin buried beneath, "Good job, kid."

She dropped down to her knees to wipe away the remaining dirt, but just before she opened it, they heard someone approach from behind.

"Saves us the trouble of digging," Sid said. Bill was quick to turn on his heel, where he found Sid with two of his goons backing him up. "You know, of all of us, I would've thought you crossing me the least," he told Bill.

"Wouldn't be the first time you were wrong," Bill said.

"I suppose not." Sid and Bill shared a lot of stories together. The *family* for the longest while was just the two of them; Bill the anchor of reality to Sid's wilder ambitions. But it seemed that meant nothing to Bill anymore, at least to Sid. "Hop on out of there, now," he instructed Abigail. "I'll deal with you back at camp." Abigail crawled out of the grave, but Bill planted his feet in the dirt between her and Sid.

"Don't be a hero, Bill."

"Just let the girl go."

"This ain't got nothin' to do with you, old man,"

Sid warned. "I'd advise against this."

"It's years' worth of taking your advice that brought us here."

"For money that's gonna set us up, mind ya. You gon' take that away from all of us?"

"I'm tired, Sid. I can't keep dancing to your tune forever."

"Certainly not forever." Sid's hand hovered over his pistol, as did Bill's and both of Sid's goons. The only one not presently reaching for their pistol was Abigail, whose gaze darted between the men to see who would draw first.

"Abigail?" Bill asked.

"Don't you be talking to her!" Sid commanded.

"Yeah?" Abigail replied.

"Run."

Bill drew his weapon as Abigail made a break for it. He ran behind her, laying down covering fire as she ran toward the church overlooking the cemetery on the hill. Sid and his goons drew their guns and fired at them. Bill took a shot and managed to down one of Sid's boys. Abigail ran up the hill, every step seemingly steeper than the last, and Bill shot the other of Sid's boys in the leg. Bill turned to face Sid, but Sid beat him on the trigger, and shot Bill in the face, sending a bullet clean through his eye. At the top of the hill, Abigail watched as Bill fell to the ground from the

shot. When Sid looked up to meet her gaze, she
quickly turned and ran past the church to the town
of Caliga Hill.

10

On horseback, Caliga Hill wasn't terribly far from the church at Reedy Creek, but on foot was something else entirely. Abigail may have been able to keep up pace beside a horse with how fast she carried herself. The acid that coursed through her veins as she forced every muscle in her body to keep up the momentum could've carried her across an entire continent. The sun was starting to rise as it became clear she was no longer being followed and she finally slowed down upon reaching the town. Disheveled and covered in dirt, she wandered into the dusty town and approached the first building to her right with a step she could take a seat on. She fell upon it, struggled to catch her breath and rested her head against the post.

Her stomach growled. Her first impulse upon entering the general store was to steal something she could eat, but if she wanted to walk a different path than the one Sid had led her down, she'd have to earn her way to a meal. She asked for work, but the proprietor had none that was 'suitable for women.' Every building she walked into in Caliga Hill, be it the blacksmith, the pelt trader or butcher; all turned her away, citing a lack of work she was qualified for. Even upon offering to dig ditches for the undertaker, something the dirt on her body was evidence of her previous experience in, she was rejected purely on the assumption she had no utility.

The consistent rejection did not do anything to undo the number Sid did on her perception of all she was good for. Despite being a crack shot and pulling her weight on every heist she rode along for, she often found herself only rewarded for what her body offered to the gang. She sat on the porch of the saloon and quietly cried to herself, sure enough that the dearth of 'women's work' in Caliga Hill might very well exacerbate her starvation and eventually kill her. *Maybe I'd be better off*, she thought to herself as she sniffled.

"You alright?" She heard a woman ask behind her. Abigail turned to see a prostitute standing in the doorway to the saloon smoking a cigarette.

"I'll be fine." Abigail wiped her nose. "Probably." Her stomach roared.

"What's your name?" Abigail hesitated when she answered. She hadn't gotten far enough with anyone she begged to work with to bring up a name.

"Clara." If she was to lay low and avoid attracting the attention of anyone whomsoever should come looking for her, at the very least a layer of obfuscation might protect her identity. This wasn't lost on the prostitute smoking her cigarette, a woman who went by the name of Dolly which, much like Clara, was not her God given name. Nadine, the head mistress of the brothel may have been the only woman who worked within its walls that had no desire to conceal her identity. Everyone in Caliga Hill knew Nadine, she'd been in town for nearly as long as the town had been around itself, and even if she didn't know it at that moment; it would be Abigail's turn now to make her acquaintance. Her stomach bellowed once more.

"You want something to eat?" Dolly asked her.

"I don't have any money."

"Don't worry about that."

Dolly tossed her cigarette and shepherded Abigail inside. The saloon was quiet; no one had stopped in for a drink just yet. The building's plain exterior belied the regal quality of the décor within. It was a nice place, run by someone who clearly took pride in their business. Dolly pulled out a chair at one of the tables for Abigail and she took a seat. She retreated into a room behind the bar, and emerged shortly after with a bowl of soup in hand. She laid it on the table before Abigail and took a seat across from her. Abigail wasted no time at all in drinking as much soup as her mouth would let her swallow. Dolly looked up to the second floor, where a hefty older woman in an ornate dress that matched the rest of the place stood, watching down on them. She nodded, and Dolly as well. Abigail was too busy hardly tasting her food to notice.

When she finally finished the soup, she sat back in her chair, and thanked Dolly for the meal. By now, Abigail noticed a couple of other prostitutes that lingered around the saloon. Abigail offered to clean as repayment for the meal, but Dolly rejected her offer.

"There's someone that wants to meet you," she suggested instead.

Abigail agreed and Dolly escorted her upstairs. The other girls all stared her down as Dolly marched her to the dressing room. The sound of muffled excitement on the other side of the doors lining that hallway peaked Abigail's curiosity, but nothing matched the sound coming from the door at the end of it. Dolly knocked on that door, and another whore answered the door. Inside, Abigail spied at least half a dozen girls prettying themselves up, with the stocky woman that had been spying on her earlier at the center of the room, wiping make up off one of the girl's face.

"You'd make more money in the circus looking like that," she said.

"Nadine," Dolly called out, and the stocky woman turned her attention to them. She spotted Abigail standing just behind Dolly. It would've been hard not to, Abigail's dirty but comparatively conservative wardrobe certainly didn't make it easy to blend into the fabric of a whorehouse.

"Hello there," Nadine said. Abigail kept her mouth shut.

"This is Clara," Dolly said. "She's new in town."

"Oh?" Nadine whistled and ushered everyone else out of the room. Dolly was the last one out, and Abigail tugged on her corset as she left.

"You'll be alright," Dolly assured her. She closed the door behind her, and left Abigail alone with Nadine.

"Sit down," Nadine instructed her. Abigail did as she was told in front of the vanity mirror closest to her. Nadine looked over the cuts and bruises that covered her body. "Nothing time won't heal," she said. She looked Abigail in the eye through the mirror. "Now I won't ask you how you got those scars, that there's your own damn business. But I will say some girls come here bringing trouble, and I ain't got the room for it. Cutting out trouble is worth ten times the money any of my girls could ever make for me. Understand?"

"Yes ma'am." New life, new Abigail. Maybe Abigail had trouble, but Clara? She could be whoever she needed to be.

"Good." Nadine started to play with Abigail's hair. "This line of work ain't for every girl," she warned.

"Well, I ain't every girl."

"That's what I like to hear." Nadine placed her hands on Abigail's shoulders. "I can't give you much. You'll have to split a room with one of the girls. Goes without saying whatever you get from your Johns goes to me first, and then you get your cut. As long as you keep working, everyone stays happy. Got it?" Abigail nodded. "Girls!" Nadine yelled. They'd all been lying in wait outside the door, gossiping over the new girl that'd wandered in but when Nadine summoned them—they burst inside, some eleven or twelve of them, and swarmed Abigail. "Make Clara feel at home," Nadine instructed. Abigail was never one to vie for the center of attention, but she certainly didn't mind her present occupation of such a zone.

It didn't take long for Abigail to enmesh herself within the fabric of the saloon. Dolly had been kind enough to offer to share her room, and the two became fast friends. The girls were a tight knit group, mostly by necessity, but they welcomed Abigail in with open arms which helped her in finding a place within her new *family*. As close as she may have become with the girls, when it came to hooking Johns in, she lacked the prowess of the seasoned veterans that surrounded her. She needed more practice in the art of separating whichever John wandered in the door with the money burning a hole in his pocket—and luckily for her, as she often would, it was Dolly to the rescue.

There were plenty of men who came into the joint looking for a girl that exuded innocence. While Abigail certainly didn't fit the description of innocent by a country mile, the idea of sharing a bed with strangers was still one she needed to break her reservations about. Dolly found and paired her up with a John willing to pay extra for naivety.

"Hey there, little missy," he said to her.

"Hey yourself," Abigail replied. She stared at the floor, unable to meet his gaze. He took her hand and kissed it.

"What's your name?" He asked. She looked up at him.

"Whatever you'd like it to be." He laughed.

"Take him up to our room," Dolly suggested. Abigail escorted him upstairs and into her room. As with anything else, whoring was a task that became easier for Abigail the more she engaged with it, and she soon became one of the most popular girls in the whole brothel. This would've been great news for her, had word of mouth not spread so vociferously throughout Caliga Hill that it brought trouble careening in through the door.

On an afternoon that began much like any other she worked, she wandered the saloon looking for her next John when a couple of men she recognized from Sid's gang walked in through the door. She turned her back to them as soon as she figured out who they were, and she walked up to the closest man she could find. He sat alone with a drink at the bar.

"How you doing, darling?" She told him.

"I-I'm doing alright." He stammered, as he hadn't ever before seen a whore that roused something within him other than blood flow. Something about her expression was inviting, like he wanted to know more of her than just her body. "How 'bout yourself?" He asked her.

"I'm feenin' for a little fun. How's about a ride?"

"Whatever you're charging, I ain't got it." She looked over her shoulder; they were fast approaching the bar.

"Lucky for you, I ain't charging." He shot her a quizzical look. She took him by the hand. "Come on, now." She yanked him off his stool at the bar, and bumped into Sid's goons as they went to take their seats. "Excuse me!" She said as she kept her head down.

"Well excuse you, little lady." One of them said.

Nadine stared her down the whole time as Abigail went straight up the stairs and dragged the man into her room. She locked the door behind her and breathed a sigh of relief.

"Truth be told, I just needed out of there," she said.

"I hear ya."

"A promise is a promise, though." She sauntered over to him. "At least you're kinda cute." The blood rushed to his face. "You're blushing," she said with a smile.

"Is that what I'm feeling in my cheeks?" He fanned his collar.

"Most likely."

"That's a first."

"Being caught blushing or laying with a whore?"

"Well—*both*."

"First time for everything." Henry may have been just another John in a long line she'd already screwed since she arrived in Caliga Hill, but for him? Clara was a godsend. As if she'd been put on this Earth for him and him alone. As they laid back on the bed, he turned to her.

"A woman's never made me feel that way before."

"You must lead a very frustrated life." She lit a cigarette.

"That felt like more than just physicality." Abigail got up off the bed, and crossed over to the divider to put on her robe. "You don't think so?" He asked, piercing the silence.

"I think you're still drifting up in the clouds."

"Maybe when you do it enough times, it doesn't feel nearly as intense?"

"Maybe." Henry rolled out of bed and dressed himself. He walked over to her and took her hand.

"Thank you." He kissed her hand. She rolled her eyes. "Take care," he said, and saw himself out.

Abigail looked down at her hand, and scoffed. She took a drag from her cigarette as she watched him walk out of the saloon and disappear down the street. Abigail kept working the rest of the day, and that night when the girls lined up to give Nadine their earnings, she realized Abigail was short.

"I saw how many Johns you took upstairs, this ain't enough," she reprimanded her in front of them all. "You trying to steal from me?"

"No." Abigail said, finding it hard to face Nadine's fury. Nadine shot up to her feet and smacked Abigail across the face.

"Let me make this abundantly clear." She smacked her again. "There ain't no free rides in my house. Do you hear me?" Abigail nodded. Nadine slapped her again. "Talk!"

"I hear you!" Nadine grabbed her by the jaw.

"Don't ever fuck me again. And that goes for all of you! You only fuck the Johns." She released

Abigail from her grasp and retired to her room. Dolly approached Abigail.

"Why the fuck are you giving out free rides? Are you crazy?" She asked her.

"I need a smoke." Abigail took out a cigarette, and kept striking the match on the box, but her hands were shaking too much for her to get a clean strike. Dolly took the matches from her and lit the cigarette for her.

"You're lucky she gave you a break," Dolly said.

"You call that a break?"

"I've seen her do worse. A lot worse," Dolly warned. It's not like Abigail got a thrill out of the job, it was purely a consequence of the circumstance, but Nadine's *No Trouble* policy made it seem to her as the only option in the interest of keeping the peace.

The next day, Abigail worked the floor as she had any other day. She was picking out her next John when she got a tap on the shoulder. She turned to meet the same man from yesterday.

"Back again," she said.

"I couldn't get you off my mind."

"That might be cause you haven't given yourself a chance to."

"I'd rather avoid that, if I can." He smiled.

"You got a name?" Abigail asked him.

"Henry. Yours?"

"Clara."

"That's a beautiful name." Repeat business is the name of the game, but she had her hesitations.

"Let's be straight—that was a one-time deal. You pay from now on."

"Understood." Abigail told him her price, and he handed her a wad of bills. When she counted it, she realized it was double what she asked for. "You earned it," he said.

She took him by the hand and initiated the ritual once again. She went through the motions as she did with everyone else, but Henry would not tire of the ride. He would return to the brothel as often as he could, only absent when he was working so he could earn a little more to give her. This went on for a period of months, and it was hard for Abigail not to form a bond with him, even if she did her best to keep him from ever learning that. Nadine had been very clear about keeping distant from the Johns, but Henry was making that exceedingly difficult. He had a good heart, even if he was thinking with the wrong head.

He lay beside her after another one of their sessions, possessed by thought. He was typically chatty as their sessions wound to a close, often looking forward more to the chance at peering into her mind than he was with the sex. All Abigail could hear were the muffled sounds of the bar beneath them, and she knew something was amiss.

"What are you thinking about?" She asked him.

"What is the worst thing I could tell you right now?"

"That you're in love with me."

He found it difficult to meet her gaze.

"That's not it, is it?" she asked.

"I'm married," He admitted.

"And?" It's not like he was the first married man she'd worked with.

"I'm married... *and* I'm in love with you."

This was it. If she was going to keep him at a distance, like she knew she needed to, she would have to tell him to collect his things, leave, and never return. Her primary concern wasn't Nadine's warning against getting too close to the John's; it was far from her mind. It was that there was something in the way he looked at her that cut through every cynical presupposition she carried of how the world worked and restored to her a sense of childlike enthusiasm for whatever surprises life might bring, as long as he was at her side when they materialized. That just his presence was enough for Abigail to ignore the red flags made him dangerous by her estimation, but she also wasn't sure if she cared. She had come to love having him around, if only for the sense of peace that he carried with him into her room.

She had been silent for a while.

"Do you want me to go?" He asked.

She shook her head. "I can't imagine ever wanting that."

They spoke for hours that night. He regaled her with stories of his childhood, growing up under the thumb of an abusive father, a man Henry's own mother apologized for burdening him with. As soon as Henry could slip away from them, he did, and he'd been on his own ever since. He found it difficult to connect with people, but his current wife had been the first person that quieted the anxieties his upbringing had hampered him with and inspired peace within him. He was quick to commit but even quicker to realize the severity of his error in judgment. He found himself unwilling to let go of the reliable stability he found in her familiarity and forced himself to live in denial of the contempt that it was breeding between them. Despite how stable she may have made his life, he'd become so deadened from years of emotional starvation that he suffered from the same sense of desperation for intimacy that Abigail was plagued by. Perhaps that was the only thing the two of them ever really had in common.

All Abigail could see when she looked at him was a wounded creature, someone she wanted to nurture and care for. He admitted to her that he'd told her things in two months that he hadn't told his wife in two years, and she felt honored to have borne witness to the piece of his soul that had been neglected for so long. What she saw was beautiful, and the only thing she wanted in that moment was to care for him in every way his wife wouldn't—if only because she couldn't bear to see the man hurting. She would keep this to herself, however. The dream of this man whisking her away from the life she'd fallen into was an impossible one, she determined, and thus she could not allow herself the luxury of vulnerability. The job would consume her alive if she did.

She still felt the physical sensations, sure, and even enjoyed herself on a handful of occasions. However, the spiritual sensation that comes coupled with the act—indiscriminately passing herself around between Sid and his goons burned that out of her years ago. She became adept at portraying feeling synthetically; the nature of the profession demanded it. As she retreated further inside herself and allowed her needs to be obscured by the performance, the girl she'd trapped within herself grew emotionally emaciated from the lack of intimacy—a necessary sacrifice if she wasn't to fall into the arms of another Sid. She had a pretty good handle on keeping her most vulnerable parts hidden beneath the hardest parts of her shell, but she could never have anticipated that the girl she'd locked away all those years ago would be strong enough to claw her way the surface if only to be present in the few moments Henry laid beside her after sex. Motivated by a naïve sense of hope, perhaps, but she didn't have much else to sustain herself with down there.

After another session, Abigail smoked her cigarette by her bedroom window, stark naked. He sat on the floor beside her, naked much the same.

"Clara?" She turned to him, and felt something slide up her left hand. She looked down, and spied Henry slipping a wedding band onto her finger.

"What do you think you're doing, Henry?"

"Marry me."

"You're insane." She stood up and crossed over to the other side of the room.

"I don't want to live without you, Clara. I can't."

"You don't want to be with me."

"How can you presume to tell me how I feel when I know what's in my heart?"

"Henry, you're married."

"I haven't felt married in years."

"Look, I'll admit I've enjoyed our times together. But you don't know the first thing about me. My name's not even Clara."

"Then what is it?" He asked. She looked down at

the ring on her finger.

"What would we do?"

"We buy a ranch. Something modest. Work the land and raise our children there."

"Buy a ranch? How could we possibly afford that?"

"You've been saving, haven't you?" He was right, she may have brought it up in a conversation or two, but that he was actually listening was another quality Abigail found it hard to ignore.

"You would really want me for that?" She asked.

"I couldn't imagine asking anyone else."

She stood there in silence for what felt to Henry like an eternity. Could she really allow herself what she wanted? She crossed back over to him, and sat beside him on the floor.

"My name is Abigail."

Henry smiled and they kissed.

"Get your things," he whispered as he rose to his feet to dress himself.

"You want to leave right now?"

"No time like the present, don't you think?"

Abigail smiled and flicked her cigarette out the window.

When she was absent from the roll call at the end of the night, Nadine stomped up the stairs and beat down on the locked door to her room. With no answer, she kicked it down herself and found no one inside. She crossed the room and stared out the open window as the drapes fluttered in the breeze. She stormed out of the room and out of the saloon. In the dirt, she found a cigarette butt with Abigail's choice of lipstick staining the butt. She shook her head, and returned inside.

Abigail and Henry would be married shortly thereafter in the very same church overlooking Reedy Creek. Family on neither side would be in attendance, one of the qualities they bonded over was the lack of family in their lives, even if on one end it was self-imposed. That fact mattered little to them. They had all the family they would ever need in each other. They bought a small plot of farmable land at a considerable mark up, Henry incurring a heavy debt with the bank to cover the cost. But as it often was with young love, it mattered little to the pair lucky enough to find themselves mired within it.

Henry nearly kicked the front door off its hinges when he kicked it in the first time they entered, his arms occupied by his holding of Abigail like a coveted prize. The place was in a state of severe disrepair, but it was a project the two of them took on in earnest. God had brought them together and blessed their union; this home that they would rebuild together would be a testament to that sacrament.

As winter rolled in and Abigail's pregnancy grew closer to being due, she felt the little one kick inside her. She rubbed her belly in an effort to sooth him, or at least, she thought it might be a boy. She certainly hoped for one. She had gone for a walk around the snow covered property, expressing gratitude to God for blessing her with all she currently had. Despite straying so far from the path, and all the horrors she both endured and inflicted upon the world, things were finally starting to look up.

She stopped in her tracks when she got a sharp pain in her belly. She tried to take another step, but the cramping pain only intensified. She fell down onto her hands and knees in the snow, and crawled back toward the house, leaving a trail of blood on the snow in her wake. It was on that day both Abigail and Henry realized God had other plans for their family, and the son Abigail knew waited to be born inside her, never had the chance to do so. She cried for days, only quieting down when her face stung from the tears. When the pain finally dulled, she would start all over again. It was bearing heavily on Henry to see his wife like this. No amount of assuring her they would try again would soothe her pain, and he refused to see her like this any longer.

One morning, she awoke to find herself alone in

her bed, and alone in her house. She waited for Henry to return, bearing two weeks of his absence. Without so much as a note, it became clear that he wanted nothing to do with her and she'd been abandoned once again. Whatever hope she had left finally shattered. She took the gun she'd been carrying with her since the raid on her home all those years ago and shoved the barrel in her mouth. She pulled the trigger, but nothing happened. She tried, again and again, but the gun refused to fire. She looked in the chamber, the thing was fully loaded. She aimed the gun at the floor and it fired. She yelled in agony and flung the gun across the room.

She later tied a noose around her neck and suspended it over one of the rafters in the house. She dragged a chair underneath it and stepped up onto it. She tightened the noose around her neck and after a deep breath, she kicked the chair. It wasn't longer than a second of thrashing when the knot she tied went loose and she fell to the ground. As she lay there with her cheek pressed against the hardwood floor, she burned with rage at the thought that Sid was right. Life *was* suffering, and there would be no simple way of escaping it. She lifted herself off the floor and returned to the bedroom. She took her pistol off the floor and exited the house. She lumbered away from the ranch where she once thought she would begin her family again. Instead, she wandered away in search of a death that would never come.

11

"Good lord, Abigail." Benjamin told her. For all the times Abigail had dwelled on these memories, moments in time where mistakes bore heavy on her soul, she'd never attempted to reflect upon or even understand the continuity that stitched them together. Such a task would've proved too painful any other time, but now that she was no longer alone, what once she found daunting was now over before she'd even realized.

She looked over her shoulder, and spotted Esperanza as she peered into the living room from behind a wall. How much she heard was anyone's guess, but as soon as they made eye contact, she ducked for cover. Benjamin stood and crossed over to Abigail. He took a knee in front of her.

"All of that is behind you, you hear?" He rested his hand on her knee. "You're with family now." Abigail caressed his cheek. "I don't know about you," he said as he took to his feet, "but I'm famished. How about some supper?"

Abigail attempted to help her brother and his wife prepare the food, but they were adamant in her status as a house guest and quickly kicked her out of the kitchen. The best they'd settle for was having her set the table, which Esperanza insisted on doing most of herself. It wasn't long before they were all seated around the table for a meal. Benjamin and Suzanne took each other's hand to say grace. Abigail took Esperanza's hand in one, her brother's in the other. He led the prayer, but all Abigail could do was look around at the three of them as they sat their eyes closed, thanking God for a meal she wasn't convinced God had anything to do with. Once over, the meal began in earnest.

"So where are you two headed?" He asked them.

"Tennessee," Esperanza said.

"You've still got a ways ahead of you. What's in Tennessee?" He asked.

"My mother." Abigail stopped chewing. It hadn't occurred to her even once on this journey to ask what awaited them at the end of this road. She'd assumed someone would be home waiting for her arrival, why else would she be so adamant about returning home? Her brother was always the more perceptive one between them, not trapped in his own head as severely as Abigail, but for the thought to not even cross her mind? This gave her pause.

"It's very charitable of you to take her such a long

way," he said.

"I'm not sure charity is the right way of describing it." Had Benjamin known what motivated Abigail to go on this journey in the first place, he might do more to stop her before she could get any closer to her goal. Esperanza spied something curious in the corner of the living room, tucked away in the crevice between a drawer and the wall.

"Is that a guitar?" she asked.

"That's right," he said. "Do you play?"

"Oh, not at all."

"Ben's a natural." Suzanne said.

"I'm fine," he said with a smile. He reached over and grabbed the guitar, resting it on his lap.

"When did you learn to play?" Abigail asked.

"I actually found this on patrol years back." He admitted.

"Patrol?" Esperanza asked.

"Me and the rest of the rangers rode up on a house that'd been razed by Injuns, this was one of the few things that actually survived." Esperanza's eyes went wide.

"You're a Texas ranger?" It was like a real life hero from one of her dime novels had just materialized before her.

"At one point. But that's a young man's game." He grabbed Suzanne's hand, and they smiled as they looked at each other.

"Playing guitar while hunting injuns sounds like you're just ringing the dinner bell," Abigail said.

"I wanted them to know. If they heard our songs, they knew their time was up."

"I wish I knew how to play," she said.

"I can show you, if you like," Benjamin offered.

"Why would you wanna go and learn a thing like that?" Abigail asked.

"Why not?" What was she getting at?

"It's a stupid waste of time." Abigail said.

"Do you think everything you don't know how to do is stupid?" Esperanza asked. The air between them was thick.

"Do whatever you like, girl. I ain't your momma."

"Yeah, you aren't."

Silence fell upon the table. Abigail, sick of pushing peas around her plate, excused herself from the table and lumbered back to her room. She didn't slam the door, but with the rest of the house quiet, the sound of Abigail isolating herself echoed throughout the house.

"You two are a prickly pair," Suzanne remarked.

"She's rough around the edges, but she means well," Esperanza said. "At least, I hope she does."

~ o ~

The next morning, Esperanza and Suzanne were just about wrapped up corralling a cattle herd one of the ranch hands had driven over from another farm. Abigail limped around the ranch with Benjamin. She spotted Sable, a former slave who managed to find work on Lambert Ranch alongside her husband Jebidiah, as she loaded up barrels of wheat onto a cart meant for the nearest trading outpost.

"Daddy would be proud." Abigail said to Benjamin.

"About what?" He asked. She pointed at Sable. He laughed. Their father was vocal on several occasions throughout their childhood on the symbol of status that came with ownership of a slave. He'd always dreamed of being successful enough to afford his own to ease the workload the family had to endure, but every time he came close to saving up enough to buy one of his own, providence would strike and sap his reserves, forcing him to begin all over again. Benjamin however, approached it differently.

"She ain't no slave, Abby." He clarified. "That ain't the world we live in no more." It hadn't been many years since the Civil War had ended, most of the country was still in a state of reconstruction but despite Benjamin's Texas heritage, he abhorred the practice as a slight against God. This was a mindset, admittedly, he only adopted after meeting Suzanne who helped him to see Godliness in places he'd never thought before to look. "Sable works the ranch, just the same as her husband, Suzanne, myself and everyone else who lives here. Think he might've had more of a problem with that than anything else."

"Abigail!" Esperanza shouted from atop her horse as she approached.

"What, girl?"

"Can I ride with Sable into town?" She asked.

"Absolutely not."

"Why not?"

"It don't matter why! You ain't to leave the ranch under any circumstances."

"But, I—"

"This ain't no discussion." Abigail limped away beside Benjamin. Esperanza bit her lip and breathed deep through her nostrils. She looked to the back of Sable's wagon, and noticed some of the supplies covered by a tarp. She dismounted her horse and lifted the tarp. There was enough room to squeeze in between the barrels, if one were so inclined. The prospect of being told what to do without so much as a discussion as to why lit a fire underneath Esperanza that refused to subside. She made sure Suzanne and Sable witnessed her leave the cart, only to patiently wait nearby for them to turn their backs and be presented with an opportunity to slip onto the wagon sight unseen.

Sable made it half way to Stillwater, the little

trading outpost where the Lambert ranch often sold most of its output, when she hit a bump in the road and one of the barrels cried *"Ouch!"* She brought the wagon to a stop and saw curious movement beneath the tarp. She lifted it to discover Esperanza hiding beneath.

"Girl, didn't yo momma tell you not to leave the ranch." She asked her.

"She ain't my momma." Esperanza climbed over onto the bench from the bed of the wagon and took a seat beside Sable.

"Oh, Missuh Lambert gon' be mad as hell!"

"Why?"

"That I's came all the way back with nothin' cause I got's to take you back."

"Are you closer to the ranch, or the outpost?"

"Somewhere's in the middle."

"Then you're halfway there. No sense in not finishing what you started." Sable bit her lip. The girl had a point. They were burning daylight every second she toiled over what to do next. She shook her head, prayed for an expedient journey, took the reins in hand and continued onward.

As they arrived at the general store, Sable met the gaze of a pair of old white men sitting on rocking chairs on a porch across the street, neither too keen on seeing her holding the reins of the cart. One of them spit as the girls unloaded the cart. Sable did her best to mind her business, making conversation about Mrs. Lambert with the shopkeeper as both girls loaded the crates they'd come to trade the wheat for into the wagon. After exchanging good byes, the two of them mounted the wagon, and Sable looked over her shoulder. The old men had disappeared.

They rode out of Stillwater and headed back for the ranch just as the sun was beginning to set. They didn't make it far down the road at all before a gunshot rang out from the trees and destroyed one of the wagon's wheels. Sable fell off the cart; Esperanza barely hung onto the wagon as it skidded to a dead stop. Out from the trees on both sides of the dirt road emerged the old men who'd been staring them down back in town.

Both sporting rifles, they approached the girls on the dirt. Esperanza tried to fight back, but the man smacked her across the face with the butt of his rifle. She fell to the ground. The other one tied Sable's hands behind her back, Esperanza's captor doing the same to her. They dragged the girls by the wrists toward a pair of horses a few yards within the trees, and threw them up on their backs. The old men spoke no words, not to them or between each other. They merely mounted their horses and nodded as they rode off together in the same direction: deep into the forest.

12

Abigail lay in Esperanza's bed, with her dime novel in hand. She'd been making the attempt, albeit unsuccessfully, of teaching herself how to read in Esperanza's absence. She wasn't going to be made the fool by some kid, even if it meant staring at that book until she could sing the words off the page. Her strained attempts at understanding the markings on the page mostly amounted to stretching out syllables that barely resembled the words written on the page, but the good news was she was beginning to comprehend.

One word though, gave her tremendous trouble: *artifact*. Something about the combination of letters in three short syllables put her through an ordeal. Granted, she didn't even know how to spell syllable, let alone know that was the word for how words were divided. Still, she laid in that bed there for a solid twenty minutes and wrestled with the book over how to say it. She slammed her fist on the wall beside her, saying *to hell with it* and electing to come back to the word later.

She would've continued to struggle through the page had her attention not been captured by the yells of a troubled man as he boomed outside. There was a scratch at the door, and she went to open it. There at her feet was Jules. The dog whimpered at the sight of her. It had been a long while since Abigail had seen Esperanza, not since this morning. She felt compelled to correct that, and exited the house to look for her. She crossed Suzanne on her way out, who lay back on the couch in the living room.

"Have you seen Esperanza?" Abigail asked her.

Suzanne shook her head.

Abigail continued out of the house and spotted Benjamin as he spoke with to Jebidiah, sporting a duster. He'd just saddled one of the horses, about ready to ride out.

"I ain't waitin' a damn second longer," Jebidiah told him.

"I'm not asking you to," Benjamin said. "I'm just saying you might wanna ride out with a posse's all."

"They're just gonna slow me down," Jebidiah said.

"I thought the same thing before I hired you for the cattle drive, lest you forget," Benjamin clarified.

It was a hard hit to Benjamin's pride to accept being led by anyone other than himself when he drove his family, cattle and everything else they had to their name further West across Texas. He'd been adamant to Suzanne that his time in the Texas Rangers meant he was more than equipped to protect them, but she insisted on hiring some extra help on the off chance something untoward should occur, at least for the journey. He ended up finding Jebidiah, then a Buffalo Soldier of the 10th Cavalry regiment. Having him along saved their skin from skirmishes with the Natives on more than one occasion, and changed Benjamin's tune. Enough to offer Jebidiah work on the ranch once it was settled, if he ever wanted.

"What's going on?" Abigail asked them.

"Sable's been gone far too long," Benjamin told her.

"When's the last you saw her?" she asked.

"This morning—loading up the cart with Esperanza," he said.

And suddenly Abigail was overcome with the notion of knowing both exactly where Esperanza would be found, but no idea where that would be.

"You riding out now?" She asked Jebidiah.

He nodded.

She walked over to another horse and started saddling up.

"What do you think you're doing?" Benjamin asked her.

"The girl's missing, too," she said.

"You're still recovering."

The swiftness with which she mounted her horse certainly betrayed that fact.

"You coming or are you just gonna keep bitchin'?" She asked him.

Jebidiah laughed as he mounted his own horse.

"I'll get my rifle," Benjamin grumbled.

Once ready, the three of them quickly rode out in search of the girls. It was some time before they'd come upon the wreck of the abandoned cart, supplies scattered across the ground and little critters scurrying away with scraps of food as they approached on horseback.

"What in God's name happened here?" Benjamin asked aloud.

Jebidiah got down from his horse and looked to the ground.

"I'm seeing four sets of tracks," he said. "Looks like there was a struggle." He continued to follow the story the dirt was telling him. He followed the track marks up to what appeared to be the prints of horseshoes in the dirt, leading deeper into the woods. "Two horses, headed in this direction."

Abigail didn't waste a second in riding out with that heading. Jebidiah quickly mounted up and followed, Benjamin close behind. They trekked forward for a good while before they came upon a secluded cabin. Two horses were hitched out front as smoke poured out of the chimney.

"Someone's home," Abigail said as she dismounted.

She landed with both feet on the ground, but such a sudden dump of weight upon her feet sent waves of pain up from her toes to her still busted ribs. She bit her lip, her determination was just that she stood and pushed forward regardless. She drew her pistol as Benjamin and Jebidiah got off their horses and readied their weapons. Jebidiah approached the door of the cabin.

"Wait a second!" Benjamin warned. "We don't know who's in there."

Sable could be, and that was the only thing that mattered to Jebidiah. He kicked the door down with as much force as he could muster, and it flew backward off its hinges. He scanned the area, but the cabin was empty. There was no fire drawn either, so where could the smoke be coming from?

"Boys!" Abigail shouted.

She'd found a hatch door on the side of the cabin with a faint orange glow flickering down below it. Benjamin and Jebidiah approached her with their guns in hand. They all looked at each other, nodded, and swung open the doors. Jebidiah walked down the stairs first. Abigail tried to follow next, but Benjamin stepped in before her, leaving her to trail in last. It wasn't a terribly deep drop to the basement floor, but every step that brought them a clearer look at the horror before them felt slower than the last.

One of the men had Sable keeled over a crate, her hands and legs tied to nearby posts. His pants were around his ankles and he thrust into her from behind as she cried. The other man stood just a few feet behind his buddy and watched. His focus was so intently upon the violation in front of him, he didn't hear the three of them enter. Jebidiah smacked the voyeur in the back of the head with his rifle. He dropped instantly, the thud catching the attention of his friend. The rapist turned around, and raised his hands at the sight of a gun in his face.

"Step away from her," Jebidiah commanded.

The man did just that, pants still around his ankles as he waddled away. Jebidiah crossed over to cut Sable loose from her restraints. The rapist eyed a shotgun leaned up against the wall nearby, but Benjamin cocked his rifle.

"Don't even think about it," he said.

Sable limped off the crate and over to the wall. She limped past Benjamin, toward the shotgun. Abigail looked in the corner of the basement behind them, and tied to a post she found Esperazna seated on the ground. She rushed over to her and cut her loose.

"We're getting out of here," Abigail told her.

"And Sable?" Esperanza asked.

Sable cocked the shotgun.

"Let's give her a minute," Abigail said as she ushered Esperanza out of the basement. They climbed up the stairs and back outside. Abigail spied the bruise on her cheek and the cut on her lip. "What did they do to you?" she asked.

"One of them hit me with their gun, but that's all," she said.

The boom of a shotgun blast echoed out from within the basement, followed by another. It wasn't but a moment later when Sable emerged from the basement, her husband's duster now wrapped around the tattered shreds of the clothes she'd left the ranch in. No words were spoken as they all mounted the horses and rode back to the ranch.

They found their way back onto the main road which took them through Stillwater once again. They continued forward steadfast, but failed to notice one of Colin's goons smoking a cigarette on the porch of the local inn. They'd managed to track Abigail and Esperanza this far, but had reached a dead end in Stillwater, staying for the night to go over what more could be done. He tossed the cigarette and ran inside.

Suzanne awaited their return on a chair on the porch. Jules sat beside her. The dog barked and when Suzanne saw them all ride up on horseback, she drew a sigh of relief.

"Can you get the boys together?" Sable asked her husband.

"Right now?"

"I wanna dance," she said.

"Anything for you, darling." He gave her a kiss. After, he turned. "Larry! Roscoe! get the goods!" He shouted as he approached the barn.

"Dance?" Esperanza asked. Had she heard her correctly? "Are you sure you're alright for that?"

"We can't let 'em take our joy for life from us. What else we got left if we do?" She told her.

Abigail too found it hard to understand how Sable managed to keep herself so collected in this moment. Had it been Abigail, she might very well be punching holes in walls if she wasn't busy trying to punch one in her own head for letting such a thing happen. Perhaps it had been the years of hardship that molded Sable's resolve into what it resembled before them. Abigail had a newfound respect for her, to say the least.

Everyone from around the ranch gathered inside the barn that night to celebrate the girls' return. Jeb and the boys played their instruments, Benjamin eventually joining in with his guitar as well. They laughed and danced and, after much goading on—they even managed to get Abigail up on the stage to sing along with them. She smiled both on the stage and off, for so long in fact, the pain in her cheeks distracted her from the rest of it in her body. If only for a moment, it seemed like everything was in its right place.

Abigail glided out of the barn and into the night air, a brief respite from all the excitement that brewed within. She approached a tree, and spotted a chrysalis that dangled from one of the branches.

"You're losing momentum," she heard a familiar voice say behind her.

She turned to see the Stranger she'd met at the train station. His presence here was familiar, but not the least bit surprising.

"What's that supposed to mean?" She asked.

"You made a promise to that girl."

"Tennessee ain't going nowhere."

"And neither are you."

"What's your hurry?"

"You wanted to die, didn't you?"

"We'll go when we're good and ready."

"You're a runner, Abigail. Always have been. Always will be."

"What do you know about me?"

"Enough."

"Abigail!" Esperanza called out to her.

She turned to face the barn and saw Esperanza approach her.

"There you are," Esperanza said. "Ben was asking

where you'd gone."

"I just needed a minute."

"Good?" she asked.

Abigail looked over her shoulder, but the Stranger had disappeared with the breeze. They retreated back into the barn and enjoyed themselves as the night continued on. After everyone had retired from the barn for the night, Abigail carted Esperanza over to her room. Jules hopped up onto the bed and curled up at the foot of it, Esperanza under the sheets. Abigail crossed over to the door.

"Sleep tight," she told her.

"Abigail?"

She turned back to her.

"I'm sorry for running off," she said.

"You understand I'm just trying to keep you safe, right?"

Esperanza nodded.

Abigail took a seat at the foot of the bed.

"If we get separated again," she said, "I'll do everything in my power to find you. But you can't stay put and pray for someone to save you. If you've gotta be the one that gets you the rest of the way home, you've gotta be strong enough to do that."

"I know," Esperanza said.

"Good night," Abigail told her.

"Good night."

Abigail exited the room and closed the door behind her. She walked over to her room and found herself quickly carried off to sleep. All was quiet on the ranch, at least—until Jules started to growl. As her growls grew meaner, she belted out a bark and Esperanza found herself rudely awakened.

"What is it, girl?" She asked, and the dog barked again.

She had her paws up on the window, stari ng out it as she continued to bark. Esperanza got up to see what had the dog so worked up only to find the barn they'd spent the night celebrating in was currently going up in flames.

13

Clint ran inside the Inn with such speed, he nearly fell flat on his face as he ran up the stairs to Colin's room. Those of Colin's gang that remained; the few that hadn't run off from this foolhardy quest to chase a teenage girl halfway across the continent, occupied each room of the building. They hadn't paid for the rooms, of course, for the meek man who owned the establishment lacked the fortitude to demand payment for the service provided to Colin and his crew. In a contest of seven against one, Colin made it abundantly clear when they arrived that the choice was obvious: endure a couple days of unpaid service, or enjoy an eternal dirt nap.

"Colin!" Clint shouted as he burst into the room. He found him kicked back in his bed, having only fallen into restful sleep for all of a minute before being awoken by his goon.

"What in the hell, Clint?" He barked as he rubbed his eyes.

"It's Esperanza." Every ounce of grogginess disappeared from Colin's person the moment her name hit his ears.

"She's here?"

"I just saw her ride on down the street with the bitch."

"Get the boys. We're leaving." Colin leapt out of bed and collected his things. Clint had half a mind to tell him that they should wait till morning, but he bit his tongue to spare himself Colin's wrath. It wasn't long at all before the rest of the gang was ready to go, they knew better than to keep their leader waiting. They mounted their horses and left Stillwater behind, following the road in the direction Clint saw Esperanza ride.

It took them some time to track her all the way back to the farm, but they managed to arrive as the party in the barn was winding down. They hid behind the trees that lined the property. Colin nudged Tim, who reached into his rucksack to hand Colin a telescope. He watched as the entire ranch poured out of the barn until he saw the one person he'd traveled so many miles to find. He spotted Esperanza as she walked beside Abigail and approached the main house.

"What's the plan, Col?" Clint asked. Colin was silent as he watched Esperanza enter the house, and lowered the telescope once she closed the door behind her.

"We wait until they're all asleep," he explained. "You guys create a distraction over at the barn while I head for the house."

"By yourself?" One of his goons asked.

"That's what *I'll head for the house* means," Colin said.

They waited there for what must've been an hour, lying in wait as everyone dispersed, returned to their rooms and the last of the lanterns were extinguished for the night. After all was quiet on the ranch, the gang began their approach. Clint took it upon himself to rile up the horses in the barn with the rest of the gang, but one of them dropped their lanterns near a bale of hay. The flames quickly sent the stack ablaze. The sound of the barn buckling under its own weight caught Colin's attention. He looked over his shoulder to see the barn going up in flames.

"Ah, hell," he muttered. There would be a change of plans, as it often was for their gang. He ran back toward the barn.

"Save the horses!" Suzanne shouted as she ran out of the house, other members of the ranch running toward the barn, some with buckets of water. No amount of water held by every pair of hands on that ranch would be enough to quell the inferno. The commotion was enough to awaken Abigail, who leapt out of bed—injuries be damned—and ran straight for Esperanza's room. When she burst inside however, neither the girl nor her dog were anywhere to be found. The drapes fluttered near the open window. Abigail ran back out of the room, to find her brother running down the stairs with his rifle in hand.

"Where's Esperanza?" she asked him as the gunshots that rang outside quickly faded into an eerie silence.

"Benjamin Lambert!" A familiar and sinister voice called out. Abigail approached the window with Ben. They found Colin standing outside the house with his men lined up beside him. Every able bodied man on that ranch surrounded them with their guns drawn, but no one would dare take the first shot. "We got your woman!" he shouted. Colin held Suzanne captive on her knees, with his gun pressed to the back of her head.

"You've gotta get out of here," Benjamin told Abigail.

"I ain't leaving you again!" She cried.

"I'm buying you time, Abby. You gotta find that girl," he told her. "Before they do."

Abigail had traveled nearly 15 years to find Benjamin once again, and once again—she was being asked to leave behind all the family she had left in the world. She hugged him, as tight as she could.

"I love you," she said.

"I love you, too." He kissed her on the forehead. "Now go!"

Abigail ran toward the back of the house and reached for the door, but she hesitated. She looked over her shoulder, and met Benjamin's eyes. He nodded, and she left. Benjamin took a deep breath and readied his rifle. He opened the front door and stepped out onto the porch.

"You Benjamin?" Colin asked.

"Indeed I am." He said.

"Where is Esperanza?"

"I couldn't say," Ben replied. Colin pulled the hammer back on his revolver.

"I'm in no mood to play games, Benjamin. I done travelled a lotta miles to find this girl. Now tell me where her and the bitch who took her are hiding." He pressed the revolver to Suzanne's temple. As strongly as she had tried to carry herself in this moment, she trembled in his grasp. If she could trade her life for the one growing inside her, she would in an instant, but she would be forced to pray that Colin might show her mercy. "We don't want things to get ugly now," Colin said.

"They left, few days ago," Benjamin said. "Didn't tell me where they were headed."

"Don't be lying to me now!"

"They ain't here!"

Abigail summited the hill that overlooked the ranch. She couldn't help but stare down at the confrontation in progress.

"I cannot abide liars, Benjamin. That I cannot," Colin told him. "It's against everything I stand for." Colin wrapped his finger around the trigger.

"Tennessee!" Benjamin cracked. "They said they were headed to Tennessee—but the girl ain't here!" And that's the God's honest truth."

"I believe you," Colin said, and he shot Suzanne in the head. She fell to the dirt and Benjamin cried out in fury. He started firing with reckless abandon, but as the outlaws returned fire and the whole ranch erupted into a hail of bullets, Benjamin ducked back into the house for cover. It would be a massacre, and all Abigail could hope to do was run.

And that's just what she did.

14

Abigail wandered the forest near the ranch, alone. She could only quiet the gnawing with Esperanza by her side. At the very least, her voice would be enough to spare Abigail the torment she'd been forced to bear for so many years. How far could she have possibly gotten? If the girl had any lick of sense, by her estimation, she would've wasted no time in moving on to Tennessee. She could just as easily still be back at the ranch, shot dead in the crossfire of the previous night or worse: back in Colin's grasp. Of any of the potential fates that could've befallen the young girl, all of them inspired nothing but dread in Abigail.

If she did fail to shepherd Esperanza back to Tennessee, what would become of her? Would she still find herself condemned to suffer eternally as she had been before their chance encounter? How was she so sure that taking the girl home would allow her the release she craved so desperately? Life could just as easily decide to renege on that promise, much as it had already reneged on the assumed promise of death at the end of Abigail's previous attempts at suicide.

She wasn't even entirely sure how a Mexican girl with a southern drawl wound up calling Tennessee home. It hadn't even occurred to her to ask, but it was only one of many other questions Abigail harbored now in the same vein. She'd been so absorbed in her self-indulgent quest to get this girl home with its implied promise of death by the end, she'd neglected to give the girl her due and now—it might actually be too late.

Regret was a common state of mind for Abigail, but this was the first time that the feeling had been so crippling, for it was her carelessness that endangered a child who didn't deserve it. However Esperanza may have regarded herself, the fact was that she remained a child; a young teenager if specifics were necessary—and Abigail had assumed the responsibility of getting her home. A responsibility she failed to keep and now suffered the consequences of the failure. It was her doing that brought violence and rage to the ranch her brother called home. Her fault that the family her brother had hoped to start once again was ripped from his arms. Perhaps he'd been spared the suffering that came with that fact with a bullet to the head, but she couldn't know for sure.

The weight of it all was simply too great for Abigail, and she began to slap herself across the face. Every hit, her penance for failing Esperanza, her penance for once again ruining her brother's life, her penance for assuming she had the fortitude to take on such a responsibility and her penance for being stupid enough to think she could ever find her. With the last hit, Abigail collapsed to the ground and cried.

As the tears rolled down her cheeks, Abigail couldn't help but picture Esperanza tied to that bed once again, how they'd come so far only for Abigail's intervention in the girl's life to make it even worse. What wrath would she be forced to endure at that animal's hands? If she could trade places with the girl, she would assume every ounce of suffering that came Esperanza's way, but such was the hand she'd been dealt, and how horribly had she played her hand.

It was the wastefulness of the journey that ate away at her. How nothing would be better as a result of all they'd gone through, and that she'd only managed to make everything worse, for everyone involved. No amount of good she may have been able to bring to those she crossed paths with would outweigh the sins against her, and she would be forced to walk the Earth for eternity with the weight of that bearing down upon her shoulders.

Perhaps it was her lot in life, to simply bring everyone in close proximity down to her level. It was no wonder she found herself isolated for so long if such a fate was what she was made for.

If only she had the chance, just one, to reconvene with Esperanza. It would be different. By God, would she do it right. If she could be blessed with the opportunity, she would do everything she could to make things right, if it was the last thing she ever did. She lifted her head off the dirt, wiping the tears from her eyes. Her vision clear, she spotted a fresh paw print on the ground—that of a dog's. One after another, they formed a trail. If Abigail was being given another chance, surely, this was it.

She followed the trail as best she could, the only trouble being that she'd kept her nose to the ground so intently, she didn't realize she'd followed the tracks in a circle. Confused, she tore a piece of her sleeve and tied it to a branch of the nearest tree. She followed in the dog's tracks once more, but when she returned to her branded tree—she cursed the day she was born. *So much for the opportunity*, she thought, but where one door was closed, another appeared behind it.

She spotted a curiosity a few feet off the ground near the tree: a spider, in the midst of repairing its damaged web. The breeze carried its strands east, almost as if guiding her in the direction she ought to go. *She couldn't be far*, Abigail figured, and she headed in that direction, leaving the branded tree behind her. She summited a hill and was able to get an eye on a good spread of the forest she found herself lost within. And that's when she found them: Esperanza with a guitar strapped to her back, Jules at her side.

"Esperanza!" Abigail shouted, elation ringing out in her voice.

It was such a strange undercurrent, at least to Esperanza, that she initially didn't recognize the voice as Abigail's. She raised a pistol as she turned to the source of the voice, but once she saw Abigail atop the hill, she lowered her gun. Abigail sped down the hill and took her in her arms. Esperanza could hardly believe the reaction.

"I was so worried I'd lost you," she told the girl.

"You? Worried?"

"I was tracking the dog's prints, but you circled around."

"To throw off the trail," Esperanza admitted. Abigail smiled.

"Good girl." They continued onward together. Abigail looked to the guitar slung across her back. "Of all the things to save, you steal my brother's guitar?"

"I didn't steal it!" She said. "He told me to keep it in my room."

"Somehow I doubt he told you to keep it period," Abigail said with a wry smile.

"It's a little late for that now, no?" Esperanza asked. Abigail had nothing to counter.

"How did you get out of there?"

"Ducked out the bedroom window with Jules. I saw the barn on fire, and when I saw who did it, I just did what I thought you'd want me to."

"You did good."

It was about sundown now, and they came upon a small lake. "This might be as good a place as any to rest up for the night," Abigail said.

"Good. I'm exhausted." Esperanza let down her things. Abigail stepped over to the lake shore.

"What say you, we teach you how to swim?" Abigail asked her.

"Right now?"

"No time like the present." Abigail took off her clothes and hopped into the water. It sent a shiver up her spine the further she submerged, the hairs on the back of her neck stood straight up. Esperanza, apprehensive at first, followed suit and took off her clothes to go for a swim. Every step she waded further into the water sent her body shaking more, but it wasn't from the cold. She got about waist deep before she stopped all together.

"You've gotta relax," Abigail said.

"That's easier said than done."

"Here." Abigail swam over to her, took her by the hand and guided her further into the water. "Breathe," Abigail said. She placed a hand on her chest. "Lay flat on your belly," she instructed.

"I'm gonna go under if I do that," she worried.

"No, you won't! Just relax. I've got ya." She held her between her hands. "Extend your arms," Abigail said. As she did what she was told, Abigail could feel Esperanza's body start to quake.

"I'm gonna sink like a rock!" Esperanza cried.

"You're going to float." She let her go.

Despite Esperanza's fears, to the contrary, she did in fact float.

"Now take your arms, and use them to pull yourself forward, like you're running on all fours."

"I'm not a dog."

"No, but your dog is doing just fine." Abigail pointed over at Jules, who was currently swimming around the lake with a smile on her face. She barked. "If the dog can do it, so can you." Abigail began to drift away.

"Where are you going?" Esperanza asked.

"Don't panic. You're gonna use your arms to pull yourself toward me."

"I can't!"

"Yes, you can." Esperanza remained frozen in fear. "You've got this, Esperanza. Swim to me."

She kicked and paddled, splashing all over the

place, but she managed to keep her head above water. Abigail caught her once she made it over.

"You see!" Abigail said. Esperanza laughed, and Jules barked once more.

~ o ~

Abigail, Esperanza and Jules broke the tree line and happened upon an abandoned town. Not a large town by any stretch, only a handful of buildings and homes on either side of what used to be a main street. The structures were rotting away, covered in overgrowth. It had been several years since this place had last been seen touched by human hands, and the tranquility of it was serene.

"This whole place is empty," Esperanza said.

"Whatever well they decided to build around must've gone dry," Abigail replied.

"You think that's what did it?"

"Could've been anything."

Esperanza approached one of the houses. She peeked in through the doorway, the door having been ripped off its hinges ages ago. She spotted a table with what appeared to be plates placed for an evening supper. Whatever food that'd been left behind by the critters that arrived in their absence was sporting mold and fungi.

"Seems like they left in a hurry," Esperanza said.

"What makes you say that?" Abigail approached the house to get a better look herself.

176

"Dinner's still on the table." Esperanza walked away. Jules began to whimper.

"I know, girl. This place gives me the creeps, too." Esperanza gave the dog a pat on the back.

"Interesting for a whole town to pick up and leave all at once." Abigail stepped off the porch. She ran her hand down the pylon, the dents beneath sparking her curiosity. It was as though someone stabbed the wood several times. There was an arrowhead still lodged in the wood, hiding beneath the vines. She removed it from the wood to get a better look, and pocketed it.

"I feel like we're being watched," Esperanza said as she looked over her shoulder to the tree line that surrounded the ghost town. The leaves and bushes swayed with the wind. "Can we get out of here?" She asked. Abigail was beginning to feel the same sensation.

"Yeah, let's go."

After they'd put some distance between them and the ghost town, they found a spot to make camp after nightfall. Huddled around the campfire, Abigail stared up at the stars.

"You learn how to play anything on that thing yet?" Abigail asked her.

"I've practiced a bit."

"Show me." Esperanza sat upright and took the guitar in hand. She strummed, note after note, playing something of a somber tune. Abigail often recoiled in the presence of music, the wrong tune would be liable to send her down a train of thought that could be too painful to endure, so she usually dispensed with music all together. Ever since sharing the stage with Jebidiah and the boys back at her brother's ranch, she no longer feared music's power over her.

"That's wonderful," Abigail said as she turned to face her.

"You really think so?" She asked. Abigail smiled. Esperanza couldn't help but smile herself, but when Abigail spotted the shadows as they shifted behind Esperanza, her smile quickly faded.

"What?"

Out of the darkness sprung a tribe of Natives. They held Abigail to the ground. Esperanza was quick to swing the guitar and it shattered as she hit one of the Natives. It mattered little though, as another came up behind her and forced her to the ground.

"Get your hands off me you injun bastard!" Abigail shouted. It fazed them little, as they continued to restrain the pair of them by tying their wrists and ankles. They proceeded to cover their heads with rucksacks, and smacked them across the head, knocking the both of them unconscious.

15

I f you had told Abigail her skull had been cracked open like an egg when she woke up inside this dreary cave—she'd have every reason to believe you. She picked her pulsing head up to spy the rock walls that surrounded her. She was tied to a wooden post, this must've been an old mine of some kind. Hard to tell, for the moon outside the mouth of the cave was the only source of illumination. Esperanza sat with her hands tied behind her to another wooden post across from her. She could just barely make out a wooden table beside them with the silhouette of a hatchet stuck in the tabletop. Esperanza awoke to the same sight, and screamed. Abigail shushed her.

"Where are we?" Esperanza asked.

"Injun territory."

They weren't alone. They turned to the mouth of the cave, where they spotted someone silhouetted against the moonlight. They stared him down in silence with wide eyes as he approached, a dog beside him. It turned out to be Jules, who walked up to Esperanza and licked her face. Abigail looked up at the native man, draped in robes with paint on his face and feathers in his hair. He couldn't have been much younger than Abigail, maybe only by a couple of years. He took a knee beside her.

"You got something you wanna say?" She spat at him. It was a long time before he responded.

"I come with an offer."

"Do I really have much of a choice?" She asked.

"Stay here and suffer the whims of the tribe," he said. "Or I help you escape."

"You help me, for what?"

"We don't have much time." The native looked over his shoulder.

"Why should I trust you?" Abigail asked.

"I am the only one who can get you both out of here alive."

"It was you bastards that brought us here. Now you're just toying with me."

"Stay here and you will die, that I can promise you. Unlike the white man, we do not break our side of treaties."

"Stop being so difficult!" Esperanza said. "He's trying to help us."

Abigail couldn't bring herself to trust a word out of his mouth but she wasn't in a position that afforded her many options. Maybe she could distract him while Esperanza escaped with the dog, but she certainly wasn't going to be able to do it with her hands tied here. Following him, against her better judgment, might be her only chance. She nodded, and he cut them free.

"Stay low and follow me," he instructed. They followed him out of the cave to see a circle of teepees a few yards beyond the mouth of the cave. As they snuck by, Abigail could see the rest of the tribe gathered in the center of the camp, engaged in some kind of ritual marked by loud drums and chants from what seemed to be the Chief at the forefront, with a large headdress adorning his head. They approached one of the teepees from the back.

"Keep watch," he said.

"What if they see us?" Esperanza asked.

"Then it's already too late." He ducked into the teepee. Abigail and Esperanza could only listen to the strange tones of the Chieftan as he delivered a speech in their native tongue.

"What do you think they're talking about?" Esperanza asked.

"How they're going to season our livers, probably." The native man emerged from the teepee once again, now sporting a satchel in each hand. He threw one at Abigail, and she caught it. She looked inside it, to find most of her belongings, most importantly her pistol.

"Come." They followed him forward, toward the horses hitched nearby. Prizes won from intruders the tribe had killed, there were only enough for each of them to have their own mount to ride upon. As they passed between the teepees, they were spotted by two tribesmen who shouted in their native tongue, sending the entire camp into an uproar. The three of them sprang to their feet and ran to the horses, Esperanza quick to scoop up the dog and seat her atop the horse with her. The tribesmen tried to grab them as they circled the camp, but they were quick to get away having escaped with their lives—a rare feat for whites that crossed paths with the tribe. They rode for hours to put distance between them.

"This is as far as we go tonight." He told them as he brought his horse to a stop.

"I ain't sleeping next to no savage," Abigail said.

"Sleep, lay awake. It means little to me. If I wanted you dead, I would have left you in that cave." He dismounted and ran his hand down his horse's mane.

"Do you have a name?" Esperanza asked him as she got down from the horse. Jules hopped down after her, Abigail the last to dismount.

"Yuma." He laid down on the ground.

"You still haven't said what you need us for." Abigail told him.

"I will need both of your assistance in performing a ritual sacred to my people."

"I'd rather avoid getting sacrificed, thanks."

"There will be nothing like that. Once we have finished, we can go our separate ways."

"Get a fire going," Abigail told Esperanza.

"No fire," he said. "Easy to spot." Esperanza looked at Abigail, and she shook her head. "We ride out at dawn." He turned over to sleep. Abigail and Esperanza sat in the dirt across from him.

"There's something familiar about him," Abigail whispered.

"What?" Esperanza asked.

"I can't quite place it." She replied. Esperanza leaned in closer.

"You don't trust him at all?" she asked.

"Not for a second."

"What choice do we have?"

"We wait until he falls asleep, then we sneak out of here," Abigail said.

"I will not stop you," he said. "But you are likely to be found by the tribe and end up back where you started. This is still their land."

"That son of a bitch heard us?" Abigail said to Esperanza, still with a whisper.

"You keep saying *theirs*," Esperanza said to him, "Like you're not one of them. Are they not your tribe?"

"They used to be. What they are now, I can hardly recognize."

~ ○ ~

They rode out in earnest the next morning. Abigail made sure to lag behind him, if only so she could keep an eye on him at all times.

"So where are we going?" Esperanza asked.

"We will ride first to the Holy Tree and collect its sap."

"What's the sap for?" Abigail asked.

"We will mix the sap into a sacred brew that will connect us to the greater realm," he explained.

Abigail laughed.

"Greater realm?" Esperanza asked.

"The plane beyond our own. This form of flesh and bone is only but a single step in the journey of the soul."

"Your English is pretty good for a savage," Abigail said.

"And your English leaves much to be desired," he replied.

"I feel the type of animals to take captive women for their sick pleasures fits the definition of a *savage* pretty well."

"You all have raped our land far worse than they could any one body."

"You're disgusting," Abigail told him.

"I doubt it changes much for you, but I refuse to

participate in such behavior." he said. "Amaru is driven more by such conquests."

"Amaru?" Abigail asked.

"He is our tribe's chief. He is also my uncle," he explained. "He's led the tribe since the white man forced us from our land. Amaru is trying to keep the tribe fed, but what he's done—he has become possessed by an evil spirit."

"What's that got to do with your ritual?" Abigail asked.

"Once we have the sacred brew, we will continue our pilgrimage to the heart of Mount Reneda." He pointed to a mountain peak off in the distance. "It is there that I hope to convene with my father."

"Your father lives inside the mountain?" Esperanza asked.

"No. My father is no longer among us. Amaru assumed his position as chief of the tribe after he passed. He has forgotten that the Earth is our mother. He has abandoned our sacred ways for the arrogance of man. The elders have more than they could ever use, while the neediest among us are starving. The tribe refuses to believe what I can see with my own eyes. My hope is to ask my father for guidance."

"Let me get this straight," Abigail said, "your plan is to drink magic tree sap so you can talk to your dead father inside of a mountain?"

"You continue to prove my point about your grasp of English, but yes."

"What a bunch of hokey Injun mysticism," Abigail said.

"Not all of us are as dead of soul as you are," he replied.

"If you go around believing trees let you talk to dead people, it's no wonder all of you are dying out."

"Abigail!" Esperanza shouted.

"Belief is unnecessary when I know what is possible," he said.

"And how do you know?"

"I have witnessed this ritual before. The sacred brew draws a bridge between our plane and the greater one, if only for the briefest of periods."

Abigail looked at Esperanza, unimpressed. They continued on their ride for a few hours until Yuma spotted something unsettling up ahead. As they drew closer, his eyes grew wide with concern and he slapped the reins on his horse.

"Hey, where you going?" Abigail said as she picked up the pace to keep up with him. Esperanza trailed close behind them.

As he approached, his fears were confirmed. A stretch of barbed wire fencing surrounded the thick woods. Nearby, a crudely hand painted sign read: *TRESPASSERS WILL BE SHOT ON SIGHT.*

"This can't be," he whispered.

"I'm guessing this tree of yours is on the other side of this fence?" Abigail asked.

Yuma was too preoccupied with the notion of being walled off from his mother, the Earth, to entertain Abigail's crude indignation. He began to ride along the perimeter of the fence in the hope of finding a better look at what was transpiring on the other side. Abigail and Esperanza watched as he rode away.

"What should we do?" Esperanza asked.

"Leave him," she replied.

Esperanza rolled her eyes and rode off in his direction. Reluctantly, Abigail followed suit. The fencing must've covered some several acres of land within its borders, as it was quite some time they rode before they got a view of anything other than a dense thicket of trees. What they did finally encounter horrified Yuma beyond belief. A logging company had moved in and begun clearing out the forest. They'd cut down enough trees to set up a trio of cabins, but there were still at least a hundred other trees that'd been chopped down and assorted. It caused him so much pain to bear witness, you might as well have asked Yuma to stare into the noon sun.

"I'm hoping your tree isn't one of the ones that were cut down?" Perhaps some optimism could be restored?

"It seems it has been fashioned into a cabin." He pointed to one of the three in the center of the clearing.

"How do you know?" Esperanza asked.

"The darkness of the bark." The cabin he pointed to had the darkest texture of the three. "It is the only tree in the whole wood with this quality and it has been ripped from its roots. Hope is lost."

"What a tragedy," Abigail said. It was clear to them both that her words betrayed how she genuinely felt. She would just be glad that this little detour was over and they could continue with their original plan. A spark of curiosity ignited within her, though, and she pulled out of her satchel a pair of binoculars to get a better look.

"What happens now?" Esperanza asked.

"To that, I have no answer." He replied.

"I'm so sorry," Esperanza said.

Abigail got a good look at the cabin in question, and noticed some movement by its front window. It wasn't long after she spotted someone exit the cabin, someone she'd seen before: none other than her ex-husband Henry. She couldn't help but laugh when she saw him.

"Do you have to be so callous?" Esperanza asked her.

"I'm not laughing at him," she said, "I'm laughing

at my rotten luck."

Esperanza didn't understand.

"If we can get you to that cabin," Abigail asked him, "can you still extract the sap that you need?"

"It's possible," he said. "However, I doubt whoever owns that cabin will allow us to rip into its walls for what we need."

"You leave that to me." She handed the binoculars to Esperanza.

"You've got a plan?" Esperanza asked, unsure with what she saw that inspired such a sudden change of heart.

"We're gonna make that cabin bleed."

16

They waited until nightfall to make their approach. Once it was clear the loggers had gone to bed for the evening, they slipped in through the gaps in the fence. Esperanza nicked her finger on the barbed wire, and drew blood. They snuck toward the cabin and hugged the side of its wall.

"Stay here," Abigail whispered.

"What? Why?" Esperanza asked.

"I'm gonna talk to them."

"That was your plan?" Yuma asked, now under the impression that he'd just signed up to be slaughtered by a mob of angry loggers.

"What's with you?" Esperanza asked her.

"What?"

"There's rage in your eyes," she said.

"I won't be long." Abigail slipped away toward the steps leading up to the cabin door. She lightly tapped it, and it quietly opened. She snuck up the stairs and gently closed the door behind her.

Inside, the cabin was dark. She saw him underneath the covers, but the darkness within made it so she failed to notice the crib by Henry's bedside, carved from the very same wood of the cabin. Abigail drew her knife from her boot, and approached the bed. He turned over in his sleep as she stood above him. She could barely make it out, but it seemed like there was someone sharing his bed. Abigail looked around the cabin and finally noticed the crib. She approached it, to find a baby, no more than a year old, peacefully asleep.

Henry's new wife tossed over on the cramped bed, now awakened from her husband's movement. She spied the silhouette of someone standing over by the crib. The moonlight that cut in from the window reflected off the tip of Abigail's blade. The woman screamed, awaking Henry and startling the baby to tears. Abigail hopped back from the surprise of it all. Henry lit a nearby lantern.

"Abigail?" How did she find him?

"How ya doing, Henry?" She faced him, knife still in hand.

"You know this woman?" His wife asked.

"I'm his wife."

"His *wife?*"

Abigail looked down at the child as it cried in its crib.

"Just leave," she told them.

"What?" Henry could hardly hear her over the

baby's tears.

"Leave. It's what your best at," she said.

Henry and his wife cautiously stepped out of their bed. His wife approached the crib and quickly scooped up her child. They exited the cabin, leaving Abigail alone inside. As Henry left, he ran to one of the other cabins for help. Esperanza and Yuma hugged the wall further into the shadows. *What the hell is she doing?* Esperanza wondered.

Inside, Abigail stared at the crib for the child that should've been hers. She picked it up and flung it across the cabin. She took out her rage on everything she could pick up, flinging things around with as much strength as she could muster. As she released her rage with reckless abandon—she'd managed to knock over the lantern, setting the whole cabin ablaze. The heat mattered little to her as she continued to tear the cabin apart. The flames crept up the walls of the cabin and enveloped her in a blanket of fire. She yelled as she took the pieces of the crib and beat them against the floor, until her hands bled from the splinters. She heaved in the center of the cabin engulfed by flames, ready to let the fire consume her, but it refused.

The wood above her cracked under the pressure of the fire, and she felt something drip onto her forehead. She looked up to see a crack in the wood as it leaked sap above her. She rummaged around and managed to find a mason jar, still intact. She took it in hand and raised it above her head to collect the sap, collecting enough to fill the small jar entirely. She stepped through the flames that covered the front door, and walked outside.

The entire logging crew stood and witnessed the cabin go up in flames. They were all struck with awe at once, like a great wind, when Abigail emerged from the cabin. Covered in soot, yes, her hands covered in blood, sure. But she had nary a burn on her body. She spotted Esperanza and Yuma on their knees with a couple of the loggers behind them. One of them had Jules on a chain. She approached Yuma and laid the mason jar down in front of him.

"This is yours," she said.

"Grab her!" Henry commanded as two of the loggers restrained her.

"Let them go, Henry," Abigail pleaded. "It's me that caused this, not them."

Henry approached her, and considered her request. He looked to the two of them on the ground, then back up at Abigail.

"Get them out of here," Henry said. The loggers forced Yuma and Esperanza to their feet, and escorted them out of the camp with Jules.

"Abigail! No!" Esperanza shouted as she was pushed away.

"You'll be fine, Esperanza. Home ain't much farther now," she assured her as she stared at the ground.

Esperanza kicked and thrashed, but remained unsuccessful in escaping their grasp.

"Tie her to one of the trees," Henry told his men. "We'll ship her off with Peter in the morning," Henry said.

"What does that mean?" Abigail asked.

"That you'll be tried in the city for nearly killing my family," Henry told her.

Abigail nodded as the loggers carried her away to her fate.

Outside the perimeter of the camp, the loggers restraining Yuma and Esperanza threw them to the ground. They released Jules from her leash and she growled at them as they left. Yuma dusted himself off and walked back toward the horses they'd left behind.

"Where are you going?" Esperanza asked him.

"To Mount Reneda," he replied.

"We can't leave her there!"

"The woman walked through fire. She can survive anything."

Esperanza rushed over and stopped him in his tracks.

"I can't do this alone," she pleaded.

"You would risk your life for this woman?"

"She's the only person I've ever met worth doing so." There was a long silence between them.

"What will you need of me?"

~ ∘ ~

Esperanza kept awake for most of the night as she monitored Abigail through her binoculars outside the camp. She'd dozed off on more than a couple occasions, but she had to make sure the loggers hadn't made good on the sign' b s promise of shooting trespassers. By the time morning broke, she'd been jostled awake by Yuma, who sat beside her with his legs crossed.

"They're moving her," he said.

She could see them loading Abigail into the back of a closed wooden cart, her hands tied at the wrists. They bolted the door shut with a padlock, and handed the driver the key.

"What is your plan?" He asked.

"Get on your horse and follow me."

Peter rolled out of the logging camp, unaware of what awaited him further on down the road. Once he was out of shouting distance from the camp, Esperanza and Yuma rode up alongside him on their horses and covered him from both sides. Peter looked to his left to see him, and to his right to see her. Down at her side, Jules chased along on foot. He watched as Esperanza lagged behind him, only to turn back to his left and see Yuma get close enough to him to spook his horse and send the cart careening off the road. What they hadn't accounted for was the dip up ahead, which sent the cart tumbling down onto its side and shattering it. As Peter managed to crawl out from the wreckage, Esperanza and Yuma stood above him.

"Is this a robbery?" He asked them.

Before Esperanza could even answer, Abigail's foot exploded through a crack in the debris. She kicked the boards around until she could slide out. Covered in cuts, she took to her feet and joined the two of them. She held out her wrists, and Yuma cut her free.

"My gun," she demanded. Peter unholstered her weapon and handed it up to her. "Get out of here."

He took to his feet and mounted the horse that had been dragging the cart. He rode back toward the camp. Abigail turned to Yuma.

"You came back for me," she told him.

"It was her that put this together." He pointed at Esperanza.

"I told you to go home," Abigail said.

"I wasn't about to leave you behind if I could help it." Abigail gave her a hug. As they embraced, Jules whimpered.

"Where's that dog?" Abigail asked.

Jules's whimpers grew louder and more strained as they searched the wreckage, only to discover the dog buried beneath what remained of the cart. Esperanza was quick to clear the debris, but when they finally got to Jules underneath, they found her injured severely—bleeding from multiple wounds. Esperanza dropped to her knees beside her. Just to whimper was a strain on the poor creature. It was clear these were not wounds she would come back from. Abigail took a knee beside Esperanza and gently patted the dog. She rose to her feet and aimed her gun at Jules's head.

"No." Esperanza said.

"We can't leave her like this," Abigail said.

"We won't." Esperanza took the gun from Abigail's hands.

"You don't have to do this," Abigail said.

"I do."

Abigail nodded and walked away to give her a moment. Esperanza laid her head against the dog's. She took to her feet, and the echo of the gunshot sent birds flying out of a nearby tree. They dug a grave for the little one, and Esperanza planted a cross fashioned out of two twigs at the head of the grave. After their moment in silence, without a word, Esperanza mounted her horse.

"Let's go," she said.

And they rode off for Mount Reneda.

17

They made camp at the base of the mountain. Esperanza remained reticent. Abigail was desperate to reach out to her; there must've been some combination of words assorted that would fix what ailed her. However, she found herself paralyzed by the thought of her existence causing collateral damage to the people around her, people she cared for. She found herself paralyzed enough to keep quiet, if only out of fear for making things worse. Not much was said at camp that night, until Yuma broke the silence by taking a seat behind Esperanza.

"I would like to braid your hair," he told her. "May I?"

Esperanza nodded meekly.

"Death is but a door we step through when we return to our mother," he said as he separated her hair into four strands. "Our souls will wander until we find our way back to her. The three tiers of heaven: the upper, middle and lower realms, are bound together by the Great Spirit, our father the Sun." He took the three strands in one hand and tied them together with the fourth strand in his other.

"These are the ties that bind us, Prairie Flower," he said, ascribing a tribal name to her. "It is in the oneness of this union between our soul and the world that we will find the strength to carry on when those we love are no longer with us." He finished braiding her hair. She smiled.

"Thank you, Yuma." She said.

"No. Thank you, Prairie Flower," he said, "For inspiring me with your strength."

The next morning, they ascended the trail up the mountain on their horses. They came upon the mouth of a great cavern that led deep within. Yuma slowed up on his horse and dismounted. The girls followed suit. They came upon a cliff overlooking a beautiful, crystal clear spring. Sunlight beat down from a gap in the rocks above, illuminating the spring a brilliant blue. They all sat in a circle on the ground as they watched Yuma mix the sap with ingredients he'd carried with him in his satchel.

"It is important that you two remain here to anchor me," he said.

"Anchor?" Esperanza asked.

"Drifting between realms can be disorienting if one is not prepared," he said. "Just make sure I stay on the ground."

"And how does one prepare?" Abigail asked.

"A sip of this brew," he explained as he poured himself a cup, "is the closest one can come to death without slipping out of the physical realm."

Abigail snatched the cup out of his hand and drank it whole. He looked to Esperanza.

"It would seem you will anchor the two of us," he said.

"How long's this gonna take to kick in?" Abigail asked.

"There are words to be spoken before travel can commence." He explained. He looked to Esperanza and had her repeat after him, the incantation in his tribe's native tongue. He had her whisper the phrases as he lay down on his back. Abigail followed his lead and lay down beside him. Esperanza sat at their heads and continued with the ritual.

"I don't feel anything," Abigail said.

"Relax," he told her, "you must allow yourself to be carried if you wish to go."

Abigail took a deep breath, and watched as the rocks above their head crumbled and collapsed upward into the sky, giving way to a cosmic starscape of vivid colors. There was no question now that she was feeling something. It was whisper quiet in the heart of the mountain when Abigail floated out from her corporeal form. There was no turning back now. Jules's bark echoed throughout the heart of the mountain.

"Jules?" Abigail cried out. She could see her just ahead, and Abigail followed the dog into the stars.

"Mommy!" The cries of a young boy echoed throughout the cosmos. Abigail looked around her, but Esperanza and Yuma were nowhere to be found. Just beyond her reach, she could see two children beckoning to her.

"Relax!" The little girl said.

Abigail drifted toward them.

"Am I dying?" She asked them. "Is this it?"

"Hardly!" Her astral son replied.

"I want to be with you," Abigail told them.

"It is not yet your time," her astral daughter explained. "There's still more for you to do."

"The truth is a secret to everyone!" He cried.

"A secret?" Abigail asked.

The boy emerged beside Abigail's form, and whispered the truth into her ear. She couldn't help but be brought to tears, watching them drip upward off her cheeks and far into the stars. She reached out for her astral children, but the further she reached, the further away they became—and she began to fall back to the Earth. She landed in the water at the base of the cliff. At the bottom of the lake, she could see a decaying corpse with an ornate headdress surrounding the skull, feathers fluttering gently in the water. A knife jutted out of its back.

Esperanza dove in and dragged Abigail out onto the rocks as she coughed up water.

"What happened?" Abigail asked.

"You started shouting and ran right off the edge," Esperanza explained.

"You left the injun up there by his lonesome?"

"Is that how you say thank you?"

"Girls!" Yuma shouted.

They looked up to see him poking his head over the cliff edge. "Good anchoring, Prairie Flower!"

"Thanks!" Esperanza told him. She looked to Abigail. "At least he's got manners."

The girls ascended back up to the cliff edge. While the pair of them sat soaking wet, Yuma seemed at peace.

"What did you see?" He asked Abigail.

"The children I never had." She said.

"And what did they tell you?"

"Death is nothing but an illusion."

"Then you had a righteous trip!" Yuma smiled.

"If you say so," Abigail replied, still confused as to what she was supposed to glean from the experience. She was inspired however, for the first time in many years, to not resent the air that presently filled her lungs.

"What about you?" Esperanza asked him.

"My father warned me of a coming storm." He said.

"No word on how he died?" Abigail asked.

"He could not be so specific."

"Is it possible he may have died here?" Abigail asked.

"Why do you ask?"

"There's a body at the bottom of the lake," she said.

Without so much as a second thought, Yuma took to his feet and dove headfirst off the cliff and into the lake. He swam to its bottom, and spotted the same corpse Abigail had seen during her psychedelic swim. He removed the knife from the body, and took the headdress as well. He ascended with heavy steps up the same path Abigail and Esperanza took to reach the cliff once more.

"This knife belongs to my uncle," he told them. Knives were sacred items in his tribe, often fashioned from the antlers of fallen deer. Each one was crafted by its owner. When Amaru returned from the vision quest that claimed the life of his father, Yuma found it suspect that he returned with his father's knife. It was how Amaru convinced the tribe to adopt him as their chief, but with his uncle's blade currently in hand, this was all Yuma needed to sway the tribe.

"Does that mean he killed him?" Abigail asked.

"It's as close to proof of his deed as I need," he said.

They followed the mountain trail on their horses, back down to a fork.

"This is where we part ways," Yuma said.

"You don't want us to go with you?" Esperanza asked.

"I have what I need, however I cannot account for Amaru's actions once I return. There's no need to endanger you both any further."

"What if they don't believe you?" Abigail asked.

"Then my tribe is truly dead, and there is nothing left to save," he said. "I have hope, though. And I have you both to thank for that."

"I was wrong about you, Yuma," Abigail told him. "You're alright."

"May the wind guide you home safely," he said.

"Likewise," Abigail replied.

Yuma continued on down the trail, back toward his tribe with the truth in hand. Abigail and Esperanza watched him as he rode.

"Memphis ain't far now," Abigail told her. "You ready?"

Esperanza nodded and they continued forward. A cold breeze blew in as their journey carried them East.

18

The snow fell gently upon them as they crossed the border into Tennessee. It had been nearly 2,000 miles they'd traveled to get here, and Abigail felt a sudden sense of emptiness wash over her as they made their approach. Would she finally be free? Or, perhaps worse, did she even want such a thing anymore? They rode up a hill to see the homestead down below on a big plot of land covered in a thick blanket of snow.

"That's it," Esperanza said.

All was quiet. They rode down the hill and made their approach. Abigail looked around and spotted broken windows, bent boards and found the house in a general state of disrepair. This farm may have been prosperous at some point, but that must've been long ago. One's first thought would chalk that up to the season, but it was clear from how badly it was falling apart that it'd been a year or more since any upkeep had been done on the property.

"You sure someone lives here?" Abigail asked her.

"We used to," she replied.

They approached the house and hitched their horses to the rotting railing of the dilapidated porch. They dismounted and Esperanza took heavy steps in the snow toward the front door. Abigail trailed close behind her. As Esperanza reached out to open the door, she hesitated.

"What's wrong?" Abigail asked.

Esperanza turned and gave Abigail a hug.

"Thank you," she said.

Abigail rested her hand upon the girl's head, and held her close.

"Go on," she told her.

Esperanza turned back toward the door and entered the house. As the door swung open, now unsettled dust glimmered in the newly let in light. The house was cold. Silent.

"Ma?" she called out.

There was no answer.

"Ma!" She called out again. She stepped further inside, and searched the house for any indication of her mother.

Abigail entered behind her and surveyed the scene. An icy breeze blew in through the broken windows. It was clear to her that whoever lived here hadn't for a long while now. She looked down at the floor and noticed a stain. She took a knee to inspect it, and from the looks of it, she gathered it must've been a dried pool of blood. Esperanza returned from her search.

"What are you looking at?" Esperanza looked down to see the stain Abigail had knelt beside. "Ma!" She shouted again. She ran outside.

"Esperanza!" Abigail chased after her.

"Where are you? Ma? Ma!" Esperanza cried out as she stepped through the snow.

"Your momma's dead, Lil Hope!" A familiar and gravelly voice called out.

Esperanza turned to see Colin and what remained of his gang as they stood in the snow outside the house.

"That's not true!" She yelled.

When she spotted Colin and his crew, Abigail drew her gun.

"Get behind me," she said. She shielded Esperanza with her body.

"That won't mean much, Miss." Colin told her.

"How do you figure?" Abigail asked.

"Ain't nowhere left for you to run!"

"You're not taking her." Abigail's grip on the gun tightened.

Colin laughed.

"What's so funny?" She asked.

"I admire your tenacity, darling. But enough's enough, now. Hand her over."

"Why would I do that?"

"For the same reason I followed your tail for over two thousand miles, woman! Don't be so dense!"

Abigail had nothing to say to him.

"Don't—oh man!" Colin laughed so hard he started to wheeze. "She hasn't told you, has she?"

"Told me what?"

"She's my daughter."

Abigail turned to Esperanza.

"Is that true?" She asked her.

Esperanza looked up at her, but her lip quivered, unable to admit the truth. Colin continued to laugh.

"Ah, hell! She always was a little trouble maker," he said. "Just like her Momma!"

"What did you do to her?" Esperanza shouted at her father.

"She wouldn't listen to reason, baby girl. She had to go!"

"Go where?"

"Do you remember what it was like here?" Colin asked her. "This land is cursed! It can't bear a crop. She didn't want to leave and we would've died here if it was up to her!"

"Just give me an answer!" She shouted.

"I shot her!"

"How could you do that to her?" She had her suspicions, but to hear him admit it was a different pain to bear all together.

"She was threatening to kill herself and you along

with her if I didn't stay," he told her. "Your mother was a sick woman!"

"So you gunned her down like a dog?" There would be no amount of strength Esperanza could muster to hold back the tears any longer.

"I saved your life you insolent little shit!"

"You wanted to go back to your glory days of raping and pillaging, don't feed me bullshit!" She yelled.

"Don't speak to me like that, girl! I'm your father!" He boomed. "Now get over here!"

"Over my dead body." Abigail planted her feet firmly in the snow between them.

"Suit yourself," Colin said.

He was quick on the draw and shot at her. Abigail was fast enough to shoot too, but Colin's bullet was quicker—her shot flew past his head and she took a bullet square in the chest. She staggered forward, and fell back into the snow.

"Abigail!" Esperanza cried out. She took Abigail's gun and fired at the gang, but with her attention in one direction, one of his crew was able to circle around and grab her.

"Get her out of here!" Colin demanded.

"Let me go!" Esperanza cried as she thrashed in their grasp, but she was overpowered and dragged away despite her best efforts.

It was getting harder for Abigail to breathe. She

heaved and coughed up the blood that had begun to fill her lungs. Colin stepped over to Abigail and took a knee.

"I hope it was worth it." He told her.

"It will be when she's free of you." Abigail said.

"This whole time, I've been trying to make sense of what's going on in that head of yours," he told her. "How consumed by rage must a woman be to destroy a man's family? Maybe it's got something to do with the same impulse that possesses her to burn down a house with women and children trapped inside it. The more I tried to rationalize such behavior, the clearer it became that I simply don't have the mental faculties to comprehend the psychopathically incomprehensible."

"Does it help you sleep at night to think of me as the psychopath?"

"Do you even know how many people you've killed on your way here?"

"I did what I had to."

"Then I suppose we've got that in common. I will certainly sleep easier now that I have my daughter back. Consider what I've done for you a kindness."

"Yeah?" She coughed up more blood. "How do you figure?"

"You won't have to suffer your delusions for much longer," he said.

He rose to his feet and reconvened with his

gang. They rode off with Esperanza and left Abigail behind to die in the snow. She laid there and bled out for a long while, long enough for her resting place to be covered by a blanket of snow in totality. The entire homestead was covered in a beautifully unbroken white blanket. To anyone passing by, it would seem as though it had been as undisturbed as it was when Abigail and Esperanza first found it. Something shifted beneath the snow, and out from underneath it, Abigail emerged. She struggled onto her feet, but managed to stand up straight, injuries be damned.

"What do you think you're doing?" She heard the Stranger ask her as he watched her from the porch.

"I have to save her," she told him.

"You've played your part," he said. "Is this not what you wanted?"

"I can't rest until she's safe." She staggered over to her horse.

"She never will be. Surely, you understand that by now?"

"Then I'll never rest."

"If you leave this place, there will be nothing I can do to protect you."

"What have you ever done to help me?" She slowly mounted the horse.

"I got you this far, didn't I?"

"You didn't get me this far," she told him. "She

did." Abigail whipped the reins on her horse and rode off.

The snow began to fall thick in a blizzard. She struggled to see far ahead at all. Her horse shared in the difficulty and displayed immense trouble navigating the snow as it trotted along at a slow pace. Abigail coughed and was overcome with an aching weakness. She clung to the horse's neck, but as the gusts grew stronger, her strength quickly faded. She fell off the horse and landed in the snow. Her horse ran off into the storm and left her behind.

She dragged herself on her hands and knees through the snow, but she didn't gain much ground. She looked up, and spotted a silhouette in the blizzard. She lifted her hand in an attempt to drag herself just a little bit further, but she succumbed to her weakness, and fell flat in the snow.

19

E speranza sat atop her Father's horse as he steered his gang westward. He hadn't been particularly open about where they were going, but if the life on the road they led before she'd managed to escape was any indication, it wouldn't take long for the bullets to start flying and they'd have to move along once again. When she didn't find it reprehensible, she often found it exhausting to live the way her father had compelled her to but now she didn't have much of a choice. The life she wanted back home in Tennessee was as dead as her mother, and the only person in the world who cared enough to help Esperanza found herself in the same company.

They hadn't spoken a word to each other since they left the homestead. She'd been silent for days, refusing to utter anything at all. Colin figured she was still steeped in denial that she was finally back, but even if she didn't want to speak to him, he was glad to have her back with family. Back where he could keep an eye on her, keep her safe. If she would just listen to him and stay put, he wouldn't have to resort to such actions as tying her to a bedpost while he was gone. How many nights had she tried to run off and how many nights did he find her? Would she ever learn that as long as Colin's heart was beating, he would do everything he could to protect her? The insolent little shit had no respect for the value of the sacrifice he made to keep her around. Keep her fed. One day, she'd understand. One day.

Esperanza knew that she was how he justified his wretchedness. He could rob a stagecoach or shoot someone he thought cheated at poker or sink to the lowest level of sin and wickedness as long as he told himself it was for her. She didn't doubt that he thought he might even be doing the right thing with such a justification, but she refused to be an accomplice in this. This might've been the furthest she'd ever managed to run off over several years of attempts, and she'd gotten a good woman killed in the process. She'd begun to wonder how much it would really be worth to endure further years of suffering under Colin's boot for God knows how long. She'd run two thousand miles and he still caught her. Maybe the grave was the only place he wouldn't be able to chase her to, she figured, but even then—eventually he would find his way there too.

"How long are we gonna go on like this?" He asked her as they trotted along down the dirt road.

"Like what?" she asked.

"When are you gonna learn that I will do anything for you, darling?"

"I think you've done enough."

"You may resent me, Esperanza, but I'm a family man."

Esperanza scoffed.

Colin turned around and grabbed her by the chin. "You don't get to pick your family. But you damn well do what you can to protect it." He released her, and turned back toward the road.

If this was to be her life, she thought, and it was nothing but suffering—how could the cost possibly justify itself, she wondered.

"This impulse of yours to run as far away from me as you can," Colin said, "you get that from me."

"What do you mean?"

"First thing I did when I was old enough was get away from my folks. I was always pushing 'em away, wanting to be my own man, even as a boy. It wadn't till your mother and I nearly died in a God forsaken blizzard trying to get back home to them that I finally understood what they were worth. But by that point, they were already gone. It was nothing short of a miracle you didn't freeze to death on that trip. You were just a baby. When we finally got home and I learned they were gone, and I was left with just you and your mother, I understood that life was about family."

This was the first time Colin had ever really spoken about Esperanza's grandparents to her. Her mother would tell stories about her side of the family back in Mexico, but Colin was always taciturn. Esperanza knew the house belonged to her grandparents, her mother had told her as much, but anytime she wanted to learn about them, he didn't have much of an answer to her questions. Not for desire to leave her unanswered, but a silent indictment of his lack of a suitable answer. The truth was, he just didn't know. He didn't care to, until it was too late.

"You can hate me all you like, but you will always be my daughter."

"And you will always be the man who killed my mother."

They rode in silence after that. Esperanza looked over her shoulder, back at the rest of the gang. Behind them, she saw something curious: looked like a man trying to flag them down. She could just barely hear what sounded like shouting coming from his direction, and he was waving his arms back and forth.

"There's a man back there," she said.

"So?" Colin asked.

"I think he's trying to get our attention."

He turned the horse around to see for himself, but when he finally turned, he saw no one there.

"He was right there, I swear!" she said.

Struck by curiosity, Colin and his gang trotted back down toward where Esperanza sighted the strange man. They brought their horses to a stop and dismounted.

"Look around," Colin said.

Esperanza stood behind Colin, who stood with his feet planted firmly in the dirt. His men searched the forest on both sides of the road as Esperanza quietly stepped back from him. She was able to slip away toward one of the horses and mount. She quickly darted away, and Colin turned to see it.

"Get her!" He shouted.

A few of his men mounted their horses and gave chase. Esperanza's heart raced as the horse galloped beneath her at full speed. If she could get away, she could start over; she just had to get away. She couldn't go back. She refused. Family or not, this was not the life she wanted. She looked behind her, and Colin's goons were gaining on her. How long would she have to ride before she finally found peace from her father's grasp? Perhaps to the end of her life, she thought.

One of Colin's men was close enough to roll out

a lasso and throw it at Esperanza. It took him a couple tries, but on the third, he managed to snag her and rip her from off the horse. She fell to the ground, and miraculously didn't sport an injury, but that didn't stop the force of her body hitting the dirt from feeling like she might've. They dragged her back to Colin, who proceeded to lift her (still tied) back onto his horse.

"I should know better than to trust you," Colin told her.

"Go to hell!" she shouted.

Colin slapped her across the mouth. Her lip bled. He mounted his horse, sure enough that this was just some ploy so she could escape again. The nerve of the girl, he thought. Maybe it couldn't be beaten out of her, but he would damn well try. They all rode off down the road, back West.

20

Shattered glass rained down upon Benjamin's head as bullets flew in through the broken window above. His wife had been shot dead by a lying animal but even with every fiber of his being sparked by a flaming rage, he knew that if he stepped out from cover, he'd surely join her. The barrage of bullets Colin and his crew were putting down upon the house was simply too thick for him to have a prayer of landing a good shot before his body would end up riddled with holes. He would be forced to wait for an opening, one that even as the hellfire died down, never arrived.

The bullets had begun to echo, the gunfight had moved without him. He peeked his head up above the windowsill just slightly, but Colin and his gang were gone. Bodies were scattered on the ground, and Benjamin could see plenty of his men with their backs to him, firing at what was left of Colin's gang as they rode away. It might've looked like Colin was flying through the air had it not been for the only detail his black horse didn't lose in the inky cover of night: its white mane. The bullet Benjamin intended to plant in Colin's skull would have to lay in wait for the time being in his rifle.

He exited the house and walked over to where his wife lay on the ground. Every step he took as he approached was slower, as if to delay what he knew he would find if only for that much longer. When he stood over her, he dropped to his knees. Her face was turned down in the dirt. He knew, but he had to see it with his own eyes. He gently turned her over, and her face was a mess of dirt and blood. He could do nothing to slow the tears that rolled down his cheeks. He tried to control his breathing; gritting his teeth all the while he made the attempt. He picked her head up and held it to his chest, and cried quietly to himself there for some time.

He gave himself that moment to mourn, but he knew he was not the only one that suffered a loss on the ranch that night. He laid her back down on the ground and took to his feet. They needed to identify the dead, and give them the proper burial they all deserved. As the surviving men who warded off Colin's gang returned from the edge of the ranch, Benjamin had them collect everyone who'd survived the assault to meet in the middle of the ranch.

He looked around at the devastation. The barn

had burned to the ground, but it wasn't the only building that did. The livestock pens were open, the animals they once contained scattered, a good number of them dead. He struggled with the notion that it might not even be worth it to rebuild, but after he allowed the thought to pass, he understood his duty to do so. It took some time, but everyone finally gathered around. Luckily, the casualties hadn't been too severe; but that they lost anyone at all was too much for Benjamin.

"You all have paid a price tonight," he told them, "and for what you did to protect our home, I will be eternally grateful. Some among us were forced to pay the ultimate price and for that, I only blame myself. It's gonna be damn hard to rebuild, but we will. I know if Suza—" His voice cracked. "I know if Suzanne were here, she would inspire us with her strength, to push through. We are the glue that holds this place together, and I'm asking all of y'all to be strong right now. Everyone who couldn't make it tonight needs it."

Their first task would be to bury the dead. There was a small gravesite already set up on the far end of the ranch. Every child Suzanne had birthed ended up in one of those graves, and now Suzanne along with them. They had to expand the radius of the yard from how many bodies were added from the last evening. There were enough men for each of them to dig a grave, Benjamin included. Jebidiah tried to spare him the grief of having to dig Suzanne's grave, but he refused. Perhaps some display of survivor's guilt with Sable having survived the night. They dug into the morning light, and the graves were ready by noon. Once the priest arrived that evening, they held the service, and paid their respects.

It would be a couple weeks' worth of work just to clean up the damage done by the assault, but they pulled through. It was a rough hit to Benjamin's business. It would take a clever readjustment of everything they did have on hand to get the ranch back to even a fraction of what it was producing before this had happened, but they'd come back. Benjamin didn't have the choice not to.

As he continued to dig through the rubble of the barn, he planted his shovel in the ash and wiped his brow. The sa me fire he'd been forced to quiet burned inside him. He wanted to believe that when all was said and done, Colin would get his comeuppance. He didn't need to practice wrath, he could leave that to God. Still—he found himself consumed by the desire. Jebidiah looked to him.

"Benjamin." He called.

He was snapped out of his fantasy.

"What's got you possessed?" Jebidiah asked.

"Thoughts of some wicked notion," he replied.

He tried to quiet his mind with loving thoughts of family, but as he thought that over—it occurred to him that he might be the only one left. "You know, Jeb, I buried my father, my mother. Every child I ever had. And now my wife. It's incredible, how you can build so much and still end up with nothing to show for it. Only family I got left done run off to Tennessee."

That stayed with Benjamin for the rest of the day. Even as he lay awake in bed, his mind would not quiet with the thought that his sister was out there somewhere, probably running something reckless headfirst into God knows what on her way to get that girl home. *She would need a home to return to once she was finished*, he kept reminding himself. *My place is here.* But every day that would go by, the voice that reminded him to rebuild the ranch grew quieter than the dread that washed over him about the fate of his sister. She needed a home to come back to, yes, but she had to come back in the first place. And he was gonna make damn sure of that. He refused to be the last of the Lamberts.

He readied himself with supplies for his journey: a little food, his rifle and some ammo, along with what few provisions he could carry to survive in the rough. What remained of rebuilding, he delegated amongst the men on the ranch. Most all of them had been there for several years; they could be trusted to get the place back to where it needed to be while he was gone. He would ultimately be back anyways, if there was a mess when he returned—it was well worth the peace of mind that would come to him with Abigail back home.

His plan was to stick to main roads whenever possible to keep this journey as expedient as he could manage. He would've preferred to take the train, but the line nearest the ranch had been closed for it was in need of dire renovation after overuse without maintenance during the Civil War. It would be a ride 300 miles on horseback to the nearest line that carried passengers, so he would have to get by on his own until then. He made camp about halfway down that road before he awoke to a troubling sight.

Rummaging through the rucksack beside him was a hungry, shit-your-pants massive, bear. Benjamin did as well as he could to keep silent, perhaps the beast would be content with what he found in the bag. The only trouble was that Benjamin's knife was also sheathed in that bag, which left him particularly exposed. If he could manage to slip away, he might not need it at all, but that assumed the bear would be too preoccupied with the bag to notice him.

Benjamin tried as delicately as he could to crawl away from the bear, but he didn't make it more than a few inches before the bear removed its snout from the bag. Benjamin stayed deathly still. The bear lumbered over to him, front paws planted over each one of his shoulders. Drool dripped down from its mouth as it hovered inches over Benjamin's face. He held his breath with his eyes shut, praying that the bear would not feel the tremors shooting across his body. He held his breath there for what felt like an eternity, and when he could no longer take it, he gasped for air and the bear swatted him across the chest with its colossal paw.

It started to bite into his chest and Benjamin yelled. He punched the bear in the side of the head which gave him enough time to roll to the side and grab the bag. As he rose to his feet with the bag in hand, he started to run but the bear swatted at him once more, and the force of the hit sent Benjamin flying into a nearby tree. He fell to the dirt as the bear ran straight at him. It slashed at his chest once again, but Benjamin was finally able to get a hold of the knife. As the bear ripped into his chest, Benjamin stabbed the beast in the neck several times. It staggered away, but ultimately succumbed to its wounds and bled out not far from where the whole ordeal had taken place.

Benjamin could hardly breathe, and was losing blood in several places. He did his best to bandage himself up by cutting the blanket he'd brought with him into strips, but he was still in rough shape. His horse had been scared off by the bear, so he was left without transport. He'd be able to walk, sure, but not without dragging his feet. The beast had also torn through what little food he'd brought with him, so he'd have to make due with whatever he could hunt for on his own.

The decision whether to head back to the ranch or continue to Tennessee weighed heavy on him. It was about the same distance in either direction, but his chances at surviving were better if he headed back home. He turned his gaze to the East, sure that Abigail would need him, current condition be damned. He looked to the West, and spied someone riding down the trail, away from him. Hopefully Benjamin could flag them down for a ride to the nearest town, he could recuperate there. He waved his arms above his head and shouted in hopes that they would see him. As the man on the horse turned around, Benjamin saw that the man was not alone. Beside him rode several other men on other horses, but the man at the front caught his attention. He could just barely make it out, but it was a beautiful black stallion with a white mane.

"Son of a bitch," Benjamin whispered to himself.

He quickly dragged himself off the road and climbed down over a small dip to hide behind the rocky formation. As Colin and his men approached on their horses, Benjamin prayed that perhaps they hadn't seen him and would just continue on.

"Look around," he heard Colin say.

So much for *that*. Colin and his men looked around for the strange man in the middle of the road. Benjamin could hear the crunch of footsteps growing louder as they approached his hiding spot, surely he would be discovered and Colin would get another chance to display his cruelty, but before Benjamin could meet such a fate, he heard a young girl shout and a horse trot away.

"Get her!" He heard Colin shout.

Everyone chased after her, Benjamin hearing the sounds of footsteps grow quieter instead of louder. He peeked over the rock only to see Esperanza, tied up in a lasso, as Colin lifted her back up onto his horse.

"I should know better than to trust you," Colin told her.

"Go to hell!" She shouted.

He slapped her across the mouth. Her lip bled. He mounted his horse, along with his men, and they rode off. Benjamin could hardly believe it. These animals had Esperanza, and Abigail was nowhere to be found. Surely, she must've been dead already and he was in fact the last of the Lamberts. Only now, the last of the Lamberts would die over a hundred miles away from home. Perhaps now his direction was clear, head back West to Texas, but first he would need water.

He managed to find a shallow creek and crawled down onto his hands and knees to drink from it. It was dirty, runoff water, but it was the only drink he'd had all day. He was lightheaded, drenched in sweat from the wounds; he needed anything he could get to keep him going. He laid on the ground and lapped at the water when he heard a branch snap nearby. He looked up from the water, and spotted a little Native girl on the other side of the creek, couldn't have been older than five years old. They locked eyes. Out from the trees behind the little girl, a Native man emerged.

Benjamin began to crawl backward from the creek, his gaze locked on the Natives across the water. The man directed the little girl to run back to the others, and she did just that. Benjamin rolled onto his back and pushed himself up onto his rear, never turning his back to him. As the Native started to cross the creek, Benjamin failed to notice how he'd lost the rifle on the ground to the roll. He only noticed when the man had crossed the creek and walked right past the rifle on the ground. Benjamin clutched his knife as he scurried backward, but the pain of his injuries rang louder throughout his body with every inch in the direction he pulled himself. He crawled backward until he he hit a tree, and held the knife out in front of him.

The native crossed the creek and approached him. He took a knee in front of the wounded man before him. Benjamin's eyes were wide with the memory of harrowing nights on the frontier from his time as a Ranger. The Native's eyes, however, were curious. He happened upon a wounded creature who looked to be in no condition to defend himself, but he also knew that a wounded animal could often be a creature at its most dangerous. He lifted his hands and spoke something softly in his language as he slowly reached for Benjamin's arm. Summoning every ounce of strength he had left, Benjamin slid the knife past the man's hand and sliced his arm. The Native was quick to smash Benjamin's wrist with his other hand, and disarm him.

The Native took the knife off the ground and stood over him. Across the creek, three other Native men arrived, one of them sporting a regal headdress. The others held Benjamin up by the arms as the man he'd just sliced with his knife argued to the man Benjamin could only presume to be the Chief. He listened.

"He tells me you tried to kill him," the Chief said.

"Wasn't gonna let him do it first."

There was silence among the five of them. Benjamin's head hung low. He'd spent countless nights of his youth chasing Natives like these down without any guarantee that he'd live to see the sunrise. He'd reveled in the enterprise—but perhaps now was his time to pay for every Native body he racked up over the years. It certainly seemed to be the case at this point.

"Forgive me, Abigail," Benjamin whispered.

The Chief stepped toward him. He picked Benjamin's chin up, so they could look at each other in the eye.

"What did you say?" he said in English that seemed too perfect for a tribesman.

Benjamin spit at the man. The Native man with the bleeding arm punched him across the face. The Chief yelled in their language at the man who hit Benjamin.

"I will ask you once more," the Chief said in English. "Repeat yourself."

"I said *forgive me, Abigail.*"

"Abigail Lambert?"

Benjamin's eyes went wide. "Who are you?"

"My name is Yuma."

21

Abigail awoke inside of a large tent. She had no recollection of how she arrived here, as far as she remembered, she should've frozen to death out there in the snow. Yet, she found herself warm as she lay beside a small fire crackling in the middle of the space. Across the flames, an elderly Native woman sat and stared at her. Abigail sat upright.

"Hello," Abigail told her.

The woman said nothing.

"You're awake," Abigail heard a familiar voice say. She turned to the entrance of the tent, to see her brother Benjamin in a thick winter coat.

"Benji?" She uttered in disbelief.

"You just can't help but get yourself into trouble, can ya?" He asked with a smile.

"How did you find me?" She asked.

"After Colin and his crew burned down the farm, I came to Tennessee to come find you."

"Why?"

"You're about all the family I've got left in this

world, Abby. Wadn't about to leave that behind."

Abigail smiled. She asked him who they were currently sharing the tent with who still hadn't spoken a word.

"This is Prancing Elk," he explained, "she's been taking care of you the last five days."

Abigail nodded in her direction with a smile. Prancing Elk replied in kind.

"Can you stand?" Benjamin asked of Abigail.

"I can try."

Benjamin helped her onto her feet and escorted her out of the tent. It was dusk. There were six teepees around, including the one Abigail just stepped out of. She could spy a couple dozen Natives as they roamed about in winter gear.

"None of these people know you were a Texas Ranger, do they?" Abigail whispered.

"What they don't know won't hurt 'em," he said. Benjamin spotted Yuma speaking with another member of the tribe and called out to him.

"Yuma?" Abigail muttered under her breath, hardly believing the sight of him. He now sported a headdress, similar to the one she'd seen Amaru wearing as he addressed the camp back when they first met.

"Glad to see you in better health, Abigail," he said. "How are you feeling?"

"Like a pile of hammered shit."

"At least your humor has been left intact."

"What are you doing here? How did you even find each other?" Abigail asked.

"We crossed paths purely by accident. Bit of a misunderstanding at first," Benjamin explained. "Truth be told, I thought I was a dead man."

"When I understood this man was your brother," Yuma interjected, "I knew we must assist in whichever way that we could."

"But what about your tribe?" Abigail asked him.

"This is my tribe!" He said.

"Is this everyone?" Abigail looked around; there were easily less people than there had been on the night they met.

"There were some that refused to believe the truth of Amaru's actions against my father, but those who did are here with us today," he said.

"But how did you end up all the way in Tennessee?" She asked.

"We go where the land needs us, much as we did before my uncle changed that of our culture. And the land led us to your brother, who led us to you."

"I'm guessing no one's seen Esperanza." She said.

"We were waiting for you to wake up to tell us," Benjamin said.

"Colin took her," she said.

"Where?" Benjamin asked.

"I have no idea," she said.

"Might this have something to do with it?" Yuma asked as he pulled out a folded page from his pocket.

Abigail unfolded it and scanned the page. There was that word again: *artifact*.

"Take me to where you found this," she demanded.

"In your condition?" Yuma asked her.

"We don't have a second to waste."

"Are you sure you can make it?" Her brother asked her.

"I don't have a choice."

Abigail staggered over to one of the horses at the front of the camp. She managed to mount it by herself, and both Yuma and her brother followed suit beside her. They rode out, Benjamin leading them to the spot where they found it initially. Night had fallen by the time they arrived.

"It was about here," he told them.

Abigail got off her horse and looked around with a lantern in hand.

"We looked around after we found it but didn't spot anything else," he said.

Abigail held the lantern up to her head in hopes that maybe that might give her a better sight in the night. It was pitch dark, next to impossible to see much of anything at all, but she did see a strange color mixed in the brush in the dim glow of the lantern light. She approached the curiosity and found another torn page—stuck to a branch of a bush. She ripped the page off it.

"She's leaving a trail," Abigail figured.

She mounted her horse and trotted along in the direction she assumed she was being led. They continued further West and followed the trail of pages one by one for what must've been miles. All cleverly hidden as to not arouse the suspicions of her captors, had they waited for daybreak they might've had an easier time of finding the pages but Abigail knew time was not a luxury they could afford. By the time they'd arrived at the end of the trail, dawn had just broken.

They found themselves outside of an abandoned ghost town. They summited a hill to see the town below, and spotted a few lantern lights inside the windows of the houses. Benjamin took out a pair of binoculars to survey the scene. He spied Colin as he exited one house and entered another.

"It's them," he said. "What's the plan?"

"We go down there and get her out," Abigail said.

"Do we know how many men they have down there?" Yuma asked.

"Doesn't matter," Abigail said.

"It just might," Yuma replied, understanding her passion but still close to his rationality. "We can go get more men."

"We don't know if they'll still be here by the time

we get back," Abigail said.

"I count nine of them," Benjamin said as he put the binoculars back down.

"There are only three of us," Yuma said.

"Three per person, I've played tables with worse odds." Benjamin said.

"This is no game," Yuma said.

"It's not," Abigail said, "but we can handle it. We just gotta do this right."

"How?"

22

Yuma casually rode up to the ghost town on his horse, with a conspicuously shaped piece of cargo draped in a blanket over the animal's back. A couple of Colin's goons spotted him as they walked from one of the houses to the main house. They planted their feet in the ground to stare him down.

"You lost, Injun?" One of them asked.

"Not at all," he said.

"Then just what the hell are you doing here?" The other asked. They both slowly reached for their guns.

"I'm here to help a friend," Yuma replied.

"You ain't got no friends here, Injun. Beat it." Their fingers twitched over their weapons.

"Now?" Benjamin asked from underneath the blanket.

"Now!" Yuma replied.

Benjamin rolled off the back of the horse and into the snow. He threw the blanket off behind him and quickly dove for cover behind one of the houses. He laid down covering fire for Yuma as he trotted away. Yuma leaned on the side of the horse to make himself as hard to target as he could, eventually dropping down beside another one of the houses with his bow at the ready while Colin's goons were shooting.

Yuma emerged from cover with three arrows in his hand, and shot them with incredible speed and precision. He managed to hit one of the men in the face with all three of the arrows he just launched. While the other was distracted with his cohort's death, Benjamin sprung from cover and shot him in the back of the head. More of Colin's men poured out the front door of the main house, forcing Yuma and Benjamin back into cover.

Over around the back of the main house, Abigail quietly trotted up on her horse. As the gunfire continued to blast in the fight out front, she snuck inside through a backdoor in the house. Despite doing what she could to get the drop on Colin's men, the surprise didn't last long at all.

"There's the bitch!" One of them shouted.

The three men still inside turned toward her and began to fire. Abigail took cover behind a wall, but the fire they were laying down upon her was thick. Shards of rotting wood exploded past her face, she didn't have much time before one of those shots blew through the wood and into her back, or brought the whole wall down upon her. She looked up and noticed the rotting wood in the roof being held up by a single beam. She shot at it a few times, and the roof above the men's heads caved in, crushing the three of them beneath it.

Esperanza screamed upstairs, and Abigail ran up the steps to find her. She burst inside the bedroom with her revolver drawn. She found Colin standing with the young girl's throat in his hand.

"Let her go, Colin!" Abigail demanded.

"How in the hell—"

She cut him off. "I said let her go!" She pulled the hammer back on her gun.

Colin raised a gun of his own in Abigail's direction with his other hand.

"After everything I've done for you, everything I've had to sacrifice," he shouted in Esperanza's face, "you lead this bitch right to us! To your family?"

"You killed my family," Esperanza squeaked out with strained breath. Colin's grip around her neck tightened. She struggled for air, and could feel herself start to go lightheaded.

"You can walk away, Colin." Abigail told him.

"Could you?" He asked her.

They shot their guns at the same time, Abigail landing her shot square in the center of his head. It exploded in a fine red mist, but not before Colin could land a shot of his own and hit Abigail in the heart. Everybody fell to the ground. Esperanza held herself on her hands and knees and coughed as she caught her breath. She crawled over to Abigail who lay now in a pool of her own freezing blood.

"I can't believe you're here," Esperanza said.

"I had to," she replied.

"But I lied to you."

"Should you have warned me he was your Dad? Maybe." Abigail coughed. "Don't know what that would've changed."

"You still would've helped me even if you knew from the start?"

"I don't know. But when I found you tied up to that bed, I just wanted you to have a choice." She coughed again, blood spilling off her lip.

"We gotta get you some help." Esperanza tried to lift Abigail, but the pain was too much for the woman to bear.

"I ain't going anywhere, Esperanza."

"You're gonna die if we don't."

"We all have to at some point or another."

"I can't let you die," she pleaded.

"You're not *letting* me do anything." Abigail was suddenly overcome with a fever of strained laughter.

"What's so funny?" Esperanza asked.

"I've wanted to die for so many years. Now it's finally here and well—I think I've changed my mind."

"That's funny to you?"

"Just a bit."

"You might well be the strangest woman I ever met," Esperanza remarked.

She was met with nothing but silence.

"Abigail?"

No reply.

"Abigail!" She shouted as tears rolled down her cheeks.

She laid her head down on Abigail's chest and sobbed into her bloody jacket. Yuma and Benjamin burst into the room to find the girl crying over the body. How it came to be that little Abigail Lambert managed to survive for so long would forever remain a mystery. What she had been brought here to do had finally come to pass, her time had finally come and she finally found what it was she was after. She'd been pining for death for years, but she'd managed to find a family to survive her. Now surrounded by them, facing the death of the entire world around her—the illusion was broken.

Even in death, Abigail Lambert would live on.